Cage of the Red Dog

By P.D. Bruns

Cage of the Red Dog
By P.D. Bruns

Cover Design by P.D. Bruns
Edited by Paula Duncan Nongard

Copyright © P.D. Bruns, 2012
Published by Arkansas River Press
First Printing, November 2012
Printed in the United States of America.
All rights reserved.

ISBN 978-0-9829555-2-9

For information regarding permission, contact:
Arkansas River Press
http://www.arkansasriverpress.com

For my wife. She edits my life.

A note of thanks...

I am very grateful to my initial sounding boards and proofreaders, Karen, JP and Shelley.

To Paula, my first professional editor, I extend many thanks for guiding me through the grammar and structure skills I should have mastered as a teenager. Additional thanks go out to her for the constructive feedback on the story, character development and overall improved readability.

P.D. Bruns

There, but for the grace of God, go I.

-- John Bradford, ca 1545

According to the US Department of Housing and Urban Development, there were more than 640,000 homeless persons, both residing in shelters and on the streets, in 2009. Additionally, more than 1.5 million people used an emergency shelter or a transitional housing program during that year. These numbers suggest that approximately one in every 500 persons in the country was homeless, and more than 1 in every 200 persons in the country used a shelter system in some way.

While most experts agree that the greatest contributor to homelessness is a lack of affordable housing, other key causes include mental illness and substance abuse.

Homeless individuals with mental illness or substance abuse issues are often unwilling or unqualified to participate in shelter programs, leaving a transient street existence as their remaining option.

Between harsh weather, hunger, violence and the isolation of a transient lifestyle, the days of a homeless person are difficult in ways that most people should hope never to understand.

A portion of the purchase price of this book will be donated to charities providing assistance to the homeless.

P.D. Bruns

1. Before

Ernest was so angry that he was physically shaking. Even with the spring chill in the air, he knew the shaking was from his fury, not the cold, as he walked down the street toward his white clapboard house on Fifth Place. Ernest had inherited the house from his uncle a few years ago. Before Ernest lived there, his uncle had rented the house out, and as a landlord, he hadn't seen the need to paint the house frequently, or at all. So, to call the house white was a bit of an overstatement. The grey of the boards beneath the white peeling paint showed through, giving it the look of a geriatric zebra.

On any other day, Ernest wouldn't have noticed, and so it was interesting to him that through his rage the dilapidated look of his home caught his eye, infuriating him further. He could find fault and error with everything he encountered as he walked up the cracked sidewalk, past the grassless front yard, up the creaky wooden stairs and approached the dusty screen door barely attached to its hinges. The aluminum screen was mostly affixed to the rickety wooden door, with duct tape holding down frayed edges. It had sediment in all the little square holes, effectively keeping any air from passing through.

It seemed that everything he saw this evening was flawed. Everything was broken. He knew deep down that this was a reflection of himself and his attitude. He was too stubborn and a little too drunk, however, to admit the fact to himself.

1

This day, which started with the great potential of any other, had turned out to be a complete waste. Ernest had risen early and half walked, half jogged to the day labor camp on Admiral Boulevard, arriving well before 7:00am. The camp was an employment agency of sorts, located in what was once a parking lot for a tiny strip mall. The lot was a patchwork of concrete, asphalt and pot holes, surrounded by rusting, tubular steel barriers about the height of a car bumper. The lot had one entrance and one exit, with a bit of a narrow drive between the laborers to give potential employers a good view of the potential workers as they went through.

The job lot was a trading post for menial work and basic trades, asking for no background check or identification or proof of education, criminal record or citizenship. All that was required for a day job was a positive and aggressive attitude, a display of energy and the five dollar "standing fee" that Charley the gatekeeper would collect from each man as he entered the lot. Nobody knew if Charley really owned or even rented the land. He may have simply started his own business on an unoccupied and unmonitored parking lot. Regardless, somehow the employers knew that there was labor to be found here. The laborers knew that a number of potential employers would visit the place, and for a laborer to stay on the lot he had to pay the standing fee. Further, the employers knew that if Charley blackballed a guy, they didn't want to have anything to do with him. There was no point in standing on the lot without paying and being in Charley's good graces, so Ernest obediently paid his standing fee with four singles, three quarters and five nickels, gaining a nod and a smile from Charley. He then elbowed his way through the forming crowd to find a good position near the entrance to watch for the best jobs coming in. He spat on his hands, and used the spittle to slick his hair back to make himself ready to bid for work against the others. Ernest was a strong man, and he knew enough about marketing himself to make himself look good and stand out in front of his competition.

The first pickup truck that came through was looking for framers. They needed three workers to cut and put up studs in a new housing development in the suburbs. The pay sounded great at forty dollars for the day. However, Ernest knew that the employer would not be pleased with his lack of framing skills, so he stayed back out of the crowd. The employer stood on the doorjamb of his truck and pointed out three fellows from the group who deftly jumped into the back of the pickup as it motored away.

The next pickup held more promise. The man in the cab needed five men to demolish a run-down shack just outside the little town of Sperry. Once demolished, they would need to load it onto a trailer and haul it to the dump in north Tulsa. It would be thirty dollars for the day. It was not as much as framing, but still a good day's pay. Ernest muscled his way to the front, made eye contact with the driver, and made sure he was pointed out. He was the first into the back of the pickup, celebrating with the other four lucky gentlemen who had found gainful employment that day.

The truck maneuvered through the city streets, eventually turning north onto the busy State Highway Seventy-Five. The air became colder at seventy miles per hour. The noise from the wind and traffic was such that the men couldn't really talk to each other, and it wasn't until they had stopped at the job site that Ernest discovered he was the only one of the five chosen who didn't speak Spanish. The employer barked some directions *en Español*, and the other four laborers picked up pry bars and hammers, and jumped into the disassembly of the tattered building from the near corner. Ernest only followed the terse instructions through, "Mi nombre es Tom," and so he simply stared blankly at his employer, not knowing what to do.

Tom smiled and said, "No hablas Espanol, eh? Aw, that's okay, just don't expect a lot of socializing, then. Since you can't work well with the others, I'll have you hauling what they break up over to that trailer. It's a little heavier work, but if you can't understand what they're doing, you'll just have to do your part here. Put your gloves on, and come this way."

Tom showed Ernest where to put the shed pieces on the trailer, and also explained how he wanted them stacked so they would not fall off when they transported them to the dump.

"Be sure to stack the studs on the side. Later, you'll need to put them on top of all the siding and sheetrock so it doesn't blow out of the trailer while we're driving. Once you have all the flat pieces loaded, then put on the studs and smaller stuff. We'll cover it up with that tarp when you're done," he said, nodding at the blue plastic tarp in the bed of the pickup.

Ernest started the loading operation obediently. He waited for the four with hammers to finish removing a piece of siding or drywall, took it from the pile they were starting, and dragged it up onto the rusty brown trailer. It creaked and swayed on its spring suspension as he moved the weight of the boards over the axles. He watched carefully for rusty nails and other sharp remnants from the old shed, being acutely aware of the hazards around this line of work. He moved the pieces fairly quickly and was able to keep up with the demolition process pretty well.

By lunch time, the building was mostly demolished, and the men stopped their work to have a quick meal. The Spanish-speaking men each pulled a paper bag from the pocket of their coat, and began assembling their lunch with tortillas, meat and vegetables. Ernest had assembled a peanut butter sandwich this morning and had also included a Twinkie he found in the back of the kitchen cabinet over the sink. He quietly enjoyed his lunch and took a few covert swigs of his favorite beverage, Red Dawg gin. The Red Dawg was not Ernest's favorite because it was good, but because it was cheap. The sandwich and Twinkie did him well, but he really enjoyed the Red Dawg and took a few more swallows before starting back to hauling debris. He knew he should have stopped at two swigs, but they were just so good that he couldn't resist.

As he carried the wood and debris from the pile to the trailer, he found the trip appeared to be getting longer each time. The step up onto the trailer seemed to be getting higher and higher, and the trailer seemed to sway more as he walked across it to pile up the wood. With these complications, he just couldn't seem to keep up with the men doing the demolition. Their pile of debris kept getting higher and higher. As he stumbled back for another load, he was met by the stern face of his employer who snarled, "Dammit, man! You were doing fine this morning! What's your problem this afternoon? You can't keep up!"

"I dunno what cher talkin' 'bout! I'm movin' as fast as I kin! That ol' trailer is floppin' around under all that weight, an' I don't figger it can take much more o' this load," slurred Ernest through the effects of the Red Dawg, breathing the toxic stench of the cheap liquor all over Tom.

"Great! You're plastered. That's *just* what we need! You better sober up quick, or you're just not getting paid.

Dammit!" the boss-man swore as he stepped back to get a breath of fresh air.

Ernest did his best to keep his feet through the afternoon, but the other men eventually had to step in and help load the trailer so they could get the load to the dump before it closed. They wouldn't talk with Ernest during the ride to the dump nor on the ride back to the day labor camp – not because he couldn't understand them, but because he had not done his part. Ernest also knew that if they had a chance to get a job together in the future, the four Spanish-speaking guys would certainly blackball him to a potential employer. In this world, your reputation was all you had, and Ernest hadn't done his any favors this day.

As Tom dropped the men off in front of the day labor camp, he paid each of the Spanish-speaking men the thirty dollars he had promised. He then handed each of them an extra five dollars. Ernest looked into Tom's eyes knowing what he had done, and fully expected the resulting ten dollar payment.

"If the other boys have to do your work, then they get your pay too. It's only fair. Keep that damned Red Dawg away from your work. You were doing great until you started in on that," he counseled, and then drove off into the twilight.

Ernest stared down at his ten dollars, two wrinkled bills with Abraham Lincoln's image on the front, and began his walk home. He was furious at the Red Dawg. He was furious at himself. He was furious at the world. He knew that Shondra Lee would be angry with him. They needed the money to buy some food for the kids, and he had only really cleared five dollars. That wouldn't buy much. He needed some strength, some fortitude, and so he took a few more draws on the bottle of Red Dawg, shaking with rage.

The alcohol gave warmth to his belly even as it took his coordination.

The sun had passed below the downtown skyline to his west, and Ernest gazed at the full moon rising in the east. He had always marveled at the beauty of the large, orange disk rising in the evening sky. Tonight, however, it only shed light for a clearer view of his depressing life. Ernest couldn't provide for his family. He couldn't keep a temporary job, much less a regular job. He couldn't stay away from the Red Dawg. It always called him back whenever he walked away.

He turned the corner onto 5th Street as a yellow Toyota sedan slowed at the opposite corner. The car came nearly to a stop and the driver's door cracked open while the car edged ahead. Ernest saw the dome light in the car flash on as the door opened wider, then a pillowcase fell from the opening. The pillowcase rolled away from the car, then the driver slammed the door closed and sped off into the night. Ernest was uninterested at first, since it wasn't uncommon for people to dump trash on the streets of this neighborhood. However, he saw the pillowcase continue to bounce and move about even after the car was long gone. When he approached, he saw the opening was tied in a simple knot. He carefully untied it and found four short-haired puppies shivering with cold and fear. A fluffy, blondish-yellow pup looked him in the eyes and whimpered.

"I'm sorry, kids, I cain't even take care of mah-self. Thar ain't no way I could handle the likes of yer," Ernest grumbled.

Ernest knew that his kids would love to have a pet, and that Shondra Lee had often talked about getting a blonde puppy.

She would tell him, "If we're gonna get a mutt, it needs to be a blonde one." But he also knew that a puppy would just be one more mouth to feed, one more responsibility, and he couldn't handle the responsibilities he already had. If he wasn't angry enough, the situation of the puppies made him even angrier. He took one more glance inside the pillowcase and again met the eyes of the blonde puppy looking up longingly for help. Ernest paused, shook his head, and then carefully placed the bag on the front porch of the brick house on the corner. He was not sure if the old man who lived there would take the puppies in, but he did know that he would give them a better chance than Ernest could.

As he turned, the little blonde one bounded out of the bag, bashfully wagging his tail and blinking his eyes as he looked at his surroundings. Ernest grumbled again, and reached to put him back in the bag. The pup, however, had different plans and dodged Ernest's clumsy hand. After a few tries, Ernest gave up and left the pup out of the bag.

"I don't blame him none for not wantin' back in there. I just hopes he kin take care o' hisself if that old man don't find 'im," he mumbled, as he continued down the street.

That diversion behind him, Ernest re-entered his walking rage and continued to look for words to help when he explained things to his wife. He could find fault and error with everything he encountered as he walked up the cracked sidewalk, past the grassless lawn, up the creaky wooden stairs and approached the dirty screen door barely attached to its hinges. It seemed that everything he saw this evening was flawed. Everything was broken. He knew, deep down, that this was a reflection of himself and his attitude. However, he was too stubborn, and a little too drunk to admit the fact to himself. Ernest drew a deep breath, opened the door, and stepped into the warm old house.

Shondra Lee, Ernest's wife of five years, was seated on an old couch in the living room, watching the snowy image of a game show on local television. Shondra Lee was a stout woman with a pink complexion and wavy auburn hair. She was certainly not movie star material, but she was beautiful to Ernest and graceful in her own way. Like Ernest, she did not need a life of privilege, just enough to get by. Tommy, their four-year-old son, was sitting on the floor opposite the couch scribbling something in a coloring book with nubs of crayons, while Jessie, their toddler daughter, was jumping on the couch beside Shondra Lee. Jessie, clothed only in a disposable diaper, bounced and giggled, , repeating, "Hi daddy!" over and over with excitement.

Ernest worried that Jessie might bounce off the couch and land on the brick mantle surrounding the dormant fireplace, but he didn't worry enough to call the child down from the couch. Shondra Lee, constantly supportive and optimistic, smiled at Ernest as he closed the front door behind him. He let that smile burn into his memory quickly, knowing it would be gone when she found what he had done.

"Hi, Ernie!" she grinned, "We're all so happy to see you! How did today go?"

"Well, darlin', the good news is I got sum work. The bad news is that it didn't pay much of anythin'," he looked at the floor and presented he earnings, adding, "Here's whut I got terday."

Disappointment spilled across Shondra Lee's face. "Ernie! Tell me you already took out the standin' fee. Tell me that!"

"I'm sorry, Shondra Lee, I'll need ter take another five fer tomorrer if I'm gonna go."

"Dammit, Ernie!" She was starting to cry. "You and me'll not get to eat tonight. What were you thinking? Taking a job like that! You know we need more than that. For five dollars, you could have done things closer to home!"

"Well, darlin', it started at thirty dollars, but I couldn't keep up in the afternoon so the boss man docked me and gave it to the others. It wasn't mah fault, really. The 'ol boss man was really just pushing way too hard."

Shondra Lee could hear the real story coming out between Ernest's slurred words. "Ernie, I can smell that damned boss man on your breath right now. We both know you can't work when you're sipping the booze. Why did you even take that with you today? Why? We have to be able to rely on you Ernie!" Shondra Lee was weeping with the innate pain of a mother knowing she would yet again have to sacrifice her own health and comfort for that of her children.

Ernest edged closer to Shondra Lee, working to hug her and settle her down, but she pushed him away, growling, "You don't touch me. You're a slave to that gin, and you're not doing any of us any good!" She snatched the bottle from his pocket and held it in the air. "Is this your family? Is this what you work for?" she screamed as she threw the bottle across the room, smashing it against the bricks on the fireplace. "Do you see that, you bastard! Do you see that glass shattering all over the room? That's what you're doin' to us! That's what you're doin' to your family! I can't believe it! Dammit, Ernie!"

Ernest stood still, unable to act, and watched the remaining magic liquid trickle down the mortar grooves between the bricks. Shondra Lee had been angry with him before, but he had never seen her in this state. It wasn't like he hadn't made an effort, was it? He had certainly tried his best. What more could she possibly want from him? With that notion, the rage he had felt walking home boiled in his veins and Ernest found himself throwing his fist into Shondra Lee's face. He could feel the bone breaking in her nose as he struck, and then saw the blood streaming out of her nostrils to confirm the injury. Tommy dropped his crayon and stared, mouth wide open, at Ernest. Jessie lost her balance in the commotion and had fallen off the couch, fortunately away from the fireplace and the broken glass surrounding it. She began to cry, more out of fear than pain, but her shrieks simply added to the chaos of the moment.

Ernest evaluated his options, and finally settled on one of flight. He stomped into the bedroom and grabbed his heavy coat, which conveniently held his spare bottle of Red Dawg. He grabbed up a tattered photograph of his wife and children, and then finding nothing else he needed, he bolted out of the house, letting the screen door slam against the jamb on its decrepit hinges.

He stopped momentarily in the front yard, hollering back toward the house, "I'm sorry, honey! I jest cain't handle all this. I love yer all, and I know yer'll be better off without mah. I love yer all. I love yer, Shondra Lee. Ah'm so sorry I have ter go!"

Ernest didn't say any soft goodbyes to his children. He didn't say when he would be back. He just left. He didn't look back as he walked across the yard and down the street.

11

A few times before when he and Shondra Lee had fought, Ernest had slept beneath the stairs of the church down the street, and the short isolation had brought him back to reality. But he didn't stop there to cool off tonight. He didn't know where he was going. He just knew he had to go. He heard a chorus of wailing as he walked away from the house. His daughter was crying in fright from her fall. His son was sobbing, and not understanding what his father was doing. His wife was writhing in pain from the blow, hungry, and not sure how she would care for the children. Ernest just walked, leaving his ten dollars, his troubles and his responsibilities behind him. He shuffled past the rustling pillowcase of puppies, seeing only the face of the little blonde one, still trying to figure out what would be next. Ernest couldn't spare a thought about what a responsibility and burden the puppies would be. Ernest could think of nothing but himself, nothing but how badly he felt and how much he wanted another draw on his bottle of Red Dawg.

2. Introduction to the Street

About one year later ...

Sam preferred to live in the present. The future seemed remote and difficult to manage. The primary purpose of the future was to provide a time for a next meal and a place of shelter. That meal and shelter was often farther into the future than Sam would have liked, but things would happen when they would happen.

Similarly, the past was, well, the past. What could be done about things that had already happened? Sam didn't like to dwell on things that had gone right or wrong in the past, and he didn't feel the need for apologies. He didn't lament when he let an opportunity pass. He didn't yearn for the easy days when meals and shelter were consistently things of the present. Back then, they were provided for him. He didn't appreciate them, but he consumed them. In that past, he didn't worry about the future. In this present, he didn't dwell on the past. It was just the way Sam was wired.

Sam's philosophy of living in the present came largely from the fact that he had little memory of his younger years. That was the time before Sam became fully charged with his own existence. That was the time before Sam made his life on the street.

Sam's first real memories involved a simple feeling of disorientation. He became aware that the meals and shelter he had expected to be handed to him were not going to arrive. He was tired. There was no place to sit and relax, and there was certainly no place to enjoy some rejuvenating sleep. The chill of the late April evening provided an additional insult to his situation. Sam shivered a bit despite the warm coat he was now very thankful to own, his sole possession. He wasn't sure where he was going, where he had been, or where his next meal would come from. He felt the pangs of hunger in his stomach and the rasp of thirst in his throat, but wasn't sure where to turn. He had looked for his home and for the comfort of his mother, but his surroundings were unknown to him and his mother was nowhere to be found.

Sam was no more than an adolescent, and was not prepared to care for himself in the harsh environment of the street. As he became hungrier, he became emboldened in his dealings with the strangers he met. He looked for help from many people around him as he wandered the streets without direction. Some people would talk with him, but then would abruptly walk away. Others shooed him away with words and fists, and even with swinging purses and umbrellas. Most people simply ignored him.

Nearing exhaustion and starvation, Sam found himself walking across the southern side of a red brick office tower at the corner of Fifth Street and Cincinnati Avenue. The evening traffic pulsed through downtown between the timed stoplights and drowned the tap-tap-tap of his footsteps as he wandered among the commuters walking to their cars and buses. He was careful not to make eye contact or otherwise bring unnecessary attention to himself. The concrete sidewalk gave way to a grey, galvanized steel grate covering the steam pipes below the street. Walking on the grate and seeing the pipes and concrete so far below made Sam a bit uncomfortable. However, the grate was effectively part of the sidewalk and the heat rising from the pipes felt wonderful as it caressed his legs. More than the heat, Sam was drawn to a worn, blue blanket crumpled on the grate along the foundation of the tower. The blanket itself looked as if it would be useful for making a warm bed, but the bigger attraction was the faint smell of french-fries coming from the beneath it.

While Sam was not consciously aware of it, his sense of smell had become extremely sharp, even as his hunger sapped the strength from his limbs. Here, his enhanced olfactory senses had served him well, for his need for food was acute.

Wary of a bruising fist or worse, Sam quietly inched the blanket back to reveal a half dozen tepid french-fries in a red striped cardboard container. He was a bit disappointed - he had hoped for a few more - but he devoured them nonetheless. As he swallowed the last of the oil-soaked potato strips, the green glass of a beer bottle flew in and out of his peripheral vision and exploded against the building behind him. Sam instinctively jumped back from the blanket.

"What're ya doin, ya damned fool?" a voice shouted from a grimy fellow near the street. "Can'tcha see them fries was mine? I had 'em stored in muh blankit. How clear did I need to make it for ya to leave 'em be?"

Passers by on the sidewalk did their best to ignore the tiff and hurry on their way. In doing so, they gave Sam and this angry fellow as much room as possible for their discussion. Sam, being of few words, bowed an apology to the stranger and began to back away. With that, the fellow drew another green beer bottle from the canvas bag hanging from his shoulder and sailed it squarely at Sam's head. Sam dodged the missile, and the bottle sailed cleanly through a first floor window of the office tower, carrying slivers of bottle and window glass across the lobby and bringing the security guard immediately to the sidewalk looking for the responsible party.

"Now yer've done it!" screamed the irritated, bottle-throwing stranger, as he quickly grabbed the blanket he was defending. "They'll put me away for damn sure if he kin grab me!" he wailed, and began a hurried hobble down the sidewalk.

The security guard was graying and had a body shape that roughly resembled a bowling pin. He was narrow of shoulders and wide of hips, with small feet that appeared inadequate to balance the weight above. His pace was befitting of his physical condition. However, despite his sluggish gait, the guard surely would have caught his limping quarry had Sam not inadvertently taken a step into his path. The security officer waddled squarely into him, falling face-first onto the galvanized grate, his legs entangled with Sam's. Sam could see a hint of blood soaking through the knees and elbows of the security officer's uniform from the impact of the fall. The bowling pin man groaned and tried to get the breath back into his lungs.

Not wanting to know what might happen next, Sam trotted quickly down the sidewalk and around the corner before the security officer could collect himself. While he was still hungry, the feeling of the six french-fries in his stomach was wonderful. The fried potato treats were definitely worth the excitement. He smiled to himself momentarily as he walked, but then realized again that he had no place to go. Sam ducked into an alley to shelter himself from the day's cool breeze and sat down on the ground to begin contemplating his situation again.

"Are ya just plain stupid?" called the now-familiar voice of the bottle thrower. "First ya thieve my evenin' snack. Then, I thought you wuz caught til that feller plumb laid himself flat on that grate. Yer one lucky damn fool – if he'd 've caught yer, they'd be puttin' yer away for certain! Yer one lucky damn fool."

Sam located the voice behind a Dumpster across the alley and quickly stood, wary of another flying bottle. He was poised to make a run down the sidewalk to put some distance between this violent man and himself. Yet, before the first step of his sprint, the smell of french-fries floated through the air again and Sam noticed the man holding another striped red cardboard container, offering to share.

"Don'cher worry. I's outter ammo. I guess I owe yer, now," said the fellow, "since yer tripped up that ol' guard man. I'm pretty slow since I banged up my foot, and he'd 've caught me for damn sure if he hadn't taken that dive."

Sam, now wary not only of a flying bottle but also a bruising fist, timidly took a few more french-fries. Again, they didn't stay in his mouth long enough for him to taste them. The french-fries simply found their way to his stomach, thankfully providing something useful for it to do.

"Mah name's Ernest," said the man, "I guess yer'd be Sam, huh?"

Sam took a few more fries as Ernest shared more.

"Yer not very tall, but you look pretty stout," Ernest observed, "I'll wager that ol' guard man just looked past yer as he was comin' fer me and didn't realize he hit yer 'til he was soles-up."

Ernest paused and grinned.

"I'd like to see that spill again, I would. But not terday. Let's us wander down to the café to see if there's more of them fries or maybe sompn even better," Ernest suggested. "Yer look pretty lost and don't know nuthin about the rules, for certain. If yer gonna make it, I guess I'd better learn you up a bit."

As Sam had no other plans, the idea seemed exceptional.

"Yer don't have much to say, do yer?" rambled Ernest, "That's okay, I've lot 'er stories for yer. I'll keep our conversations movin'. Say, that's one hell of a nice yeller coat you have. That's gotter be handy when it's cold – bet yer glad to have 'er."

Sam didn't argue, and Ernest didn't wait for him to speak up. "Let's foller this alley. It's the safest way to git there," Ernest continued, taking a hard left onto a brick-paved corridor between some lofts.

"If we take the alley, there's not s' many cars, ya see. Them cars on the street'll getcha. One smack, and it can be all over. And even if yer not done fur by the car, the off'cers, they'll take yer to the hospital and yer'll not be back. Dunno what happens there, but I've never seen summon come back after bein' hauled off. I've been livin' on mah own out here fur more than a year, and ah've never seen summon come back. It just don't happen."

"That's wut happened to mah foot, yer know. Just a couple blocks down yonder, last week. The damn fool pulled his car into the cross walk at the red light and went right over mah foot. There was tar tracks on the top of mah boot and everythin'."

It was fortunate that Sam didn't have a lot to say, as he would have difficulty breaking into the conversation even when he did want to add something.

"Mah foot turned all blue and black – all them toes and up almost to mah ankle, but it's healin' a bit now. Ah'm happy I can put some weight on it now. Ah'm hopin I'll be fleet o foot again sometime soon! Say, you look like you might be pretty quick on yer feet."

It wasn't something Sam had contemplated. He had noticed that on those occasions when strangers were threatening, he could flee quickly and easily put distance between himself and the dangerous stranger. So, Ernest's assessment seemed reasonable.

"We might could be a good team, yer and me. I know how to work the street, and yer fast enough to get thangs done. We'll have to find some opportunities for ourselves! Let's get ourselves some working energy first and we'll figger it out from there. Up here at the café, just foller my lead – you'll figger it out soon enough. Foller me – we're goin' to dinner!"

Ernest hobbled out of the alley and dodged several swerving cars as he crossed the wide one-way street on his way to the fast-food restaurant. It was nearly empty inside, but had five cars lined up to order in the drive-through lane forming a semi-circle in the parking lot surrounding the rectangular building. Ernest grinned and pointed to the minivan idling four back in the line. The white Chrysler was relatively new, but quite dirty with the scuff marks of children's shoes decorating the body of the car below the

19

sliding rear doors. The back window had two smiley faces drawn in the dust, along with the obligatory *Wash Me!* scrawled in for good measure. Ernest could see the silhouette of the driver and a passenger, plus at least four additional passengers in the back – a guaranteed rich score!

"Awl right, Sam. That's our mark. Let's let 'em order at the intercom, then we'll meet 'em at the pickup window. I'll come in from the front." Ernest moved his hands to illustrate the path of the pair's assault on the minivan and the restaurant. "They'll see me and get a little uptight. Yer'll come around from behind. They won't see yer 'cause they'll be fixed on me. Then, yer jest wait for my sign. Got it?"

Sam did not have any violent tendencies toward people, but he could smell the hamburgers and french-fries from outside the restaurant. His stomach growled again, and so he went along, his hunger overcoming his apprehension.

Ernest and Sam stood together and watched the minivan family take their turn at the speaker. The driver was the mother, and she took some time to convey the order through the intercom. Sam could hear the children calling to her, correcting her as she worked to communicate through the static of the machine. The chaos inside the minivan brought a rare memory back from the archives of Sam's brain, forcing him to longingly recall the warmth and comfort of his mother, brothers and sisters. He came back to the present when the order was complete, and the minivan inched forward toward the next window.

"We don't go yet –it'll take 'em a minute to get their food together. I've got their timing down – gotta count from fity before we move," updated Ernest, as he started counting down, watching the restaurant employees gathering food for the bag. "… Three … two … one. Awl right, partner, les go!"

Sam obediently stepped behind the minivan, and then walked up the narrow space between the driver's side and the wall of the restaurant. He quietly brought himself just behind the stainless steel shelf protruding from the restaurant to help deliver the food to the drivers. As he did, he saw Ernest hobble across the front of the van, and simultaneously heard the chattering occupants go quiet at the sight of him. They were silenced by the shell of a man dressed in rags with two weeks of growth in his beard and two weeks of grime on the parts of his face not covered with hair.

The driver instinctively started to raise her window to avoid the inevitable conversation with Ernest, but he slowed her, "Good evening, ma'am, would you have sompn small to lend to a gentleman who's down on his luck?"

Her response was a silent shake of her head and she raised her palm toward Ernest defensively. Again, she went for the window button to raise the glass barrier. But, as the car window started up, the sliding window of the restaurant opened with the smiling face of the drive-through attendant. "Here's your order, ma'am," the pimple-faced, teenage boy stated with all the enthusiasm one would expect from an adolescent who had delivered a hundred packages of food thus far on his shift, and who knew he had another hundred before his shift ended. He placed the bag on the stainless steel shelf and opened his hand to receive payment for the food, adding, "That'll be twenty one forty seven."

Only then did the attendant notice that the driver's attention was focused at Ernest instead of her food, and Sam could sense the fear forming in the attendant's demeanor.

Ernest started his pitch again, "Ma'am, I jest could use some spare change – mebbe that fity-three cents yer gettin' back from that young man might be a nice start."

Sam now understood Ernest's panhandling was a ruse, as Ernest looked Sam in the eyes and gave him a subtle nod. At that signal, Ernest forced a violent cough and feigned a stumble toward the stainless steel shelf. As he stumbled, Ernest deftly knocked the bag bulging with hamburgers and french-fries to the ground in the direction of Sam.

"Pardon me so much, ma'am, I knocked yer stuff down. Here, let me git it back for yer," he continued, playing out the choreographed scene. Sam picked up the bag and silently sprinted behind the minivan and back to the alley where he and Ernest had rested before. He was ecstatic that he had some food, and even more so that Ernest's plan didn't require harming the people involved.

The exasperated driver perfectly concluded the scene, "No, no! Never mind! I don't want it now! We'll just go somewhere else!" She raised her window and quickly drove off, leaving only the attendant and Ernest to watch the van speed down the street.

"Many apologies, kind sir," Ernest did his best to keep a straight face as he displayed some pennies, lint and a few blades of brown grass he dug from his coat pocket, "Kin I compensate yer for yer losses? I have eighteen cents right here."

"Please just go," replied the attendant, as he rolled his eyes and slammed the sliding glass window closed. Ernest, knowing that his mission was a complete success, took his leave.

Backtracking across the restaurant parking lot, down the block, then across the four lanes of one-way traffic, Ernest made his way back to the alley where Sam was starting in on his second hamburger. Without any hesitation, Ernest swung his large right hand across Sam's chest, knocking him back against a brick wall and away from the bag of food.

"Don't yer have any manners at all, you scoundrel!" he raged. "I masterminded the whole plan and did the hardest part! The least yer could do is ter wait for fer me to split up our winnin's even-like. We could be a great team, but yer have ter think about us both and mind yer manners!"

Sam's chest ached from Ernest's blow, and his back was sore from the brick wall, but he understood what Ernest wanted and respected him for making his position clear. He walked, apologetically, back toward the bag as Ernest was distributing the food into two piles. In the end, there were two more hamburgers each, several bags of french-fries, and a box each of chicken chunks. Ernest started on his pile. Sam started only after Ernest motioned his permission and forgiveness. The alley was silent as they filled their aching stomachs, and remained quiet until no crumbs remained. While it all tasted great, Sam enjoyed the chicken chunks most of all and noted them as a most excellent prize. When the food was gone and their stomachs were full, they sat next to the brick wall to relax.

"I'm sorry about hittin' yer," said Ernest, "but yer do need to learn your manners."

Sam understood.

"We're gonna make a great team, yer know. I'm smart and can figger how thangs work. I kin find us opportunities,"

Ernest jabbered on, "Yer quick and quiet, and I think yer can learn up pretty fast. We kin take care of each other. We'll find *opportunities!*" Ernest smiled.

Sam was okay with that.

"That ol' café will post a guard man by the drive through now. Probly stay there for a couple weeks. We'll have to find sompn else next. That's what they always do. Let's find us a place to bed up for the night. I got some blankets in my pack, so I'll share with yer. I gotta place in mind. We'll git some good sleep."

Sam followed Ernest as they traveled down the alley to another wide one-way street. It led to a long and tall parabolic bridge over ten sets of railroad tracks, with a convenient sidewalk alongside. No trains moved on the tracks while they crossed over the bridge, but Sam could tell that this was a place of some significant activity, as there were still several workers near the tracks even at this hour of the evening. The pair reached the far side of the bridge and Ernest began studying the chain link fence surrounding it, apparently looking for just the right place to stop.

When they came to that place, evidenced by a small gap, Ernest first looked all around them on the street. Seeing no one but busy commuters in their sedans zipping down the bridge on their way to the suburbs, Ernest gently pulled the chain link back revealing an opening just large enough for the pair to fit through and step down to the ground below the bridge. Ernest carefully put the chain link back in place so that only a very keen eye would see the gap. He looked all around the area beneath the bridge, seeing only the railroad workers out on the tracks, likely inspecting the area for the next set of trains due to come through. Weeds, awakened by the wet and warming April weather, were already popping up and beginning to line the tracks with a green border.

"Come on!" whispered Ernest, and Sam followed. Ernest stepped back under the bridge and stopped at a flat pad of concrete, slightly raised above the ground and large enough for both of them to stretch out.

"This spot is great because it's raised up, it's covered, and it's flat. The flat is great for sleeping, and if it rains, we won't get wet because it's both covered and it's raised up! I haven't told no one 'bout it cuz somebody would git caught here and then the railroad would fix that there hole in the fence. Don't yer tell nobody neither, ya hear? And don't yer get caught comin' or goin'. It's a special place and I don't want ter lose 'er to the railroaders closin' 'er down or to another guy sleepin' *rough*. I'm only sharin' it with yer cause we're a team."

The sun had long since set, yet the glow of the bright downtown lights provided just enough visibility beneath the bridge to get comfortable on the concrete pad. Ernest opened his pack, which housed all of his worldly belongings, and took a quick inventory.

"Here's mah blankets. I got five of 'em, so I usually sleep on three and put two on top of me. Yer kin have this one, so I'll just sleep on two tonight. I kin see that yer have a great-looking coat, so I think yer should just sleep on that blanket as a pad."

Sam settled in on the blanket and admired his coat. He had really taken it for granted, but Ernest was right – it was a nice coat and did a good job keeping him warm.

"This is mah Bible. It ain't the whole thang, but it's the most important parts. I got most of Habakuk through Malachi in the Old Testament, along with Matthew through Ephesians in the New Testament. I don't need no Genesis, since I knows how God created this Earth. Ah'd like to have me some Revelation, though, cuz the Revelation lays out how the world ends. But, I just ain't got it here. Ah'm hopin' that the world don't end 'til ah've found me a Revelation. The rev'rend tells me that the answers I need are right in this here book. I believe I just needs to find 'em between the words." Ernest took a deep breath as he stared at the pages of his bible. "Hell! I'll read this 'til kingdom come and still won't get it all!"

"Ah've got lots of little thangs too. Here's mah extra gloves. They don't match, but I kin wear 'em under these when it's really cold. I also have an extra sock. I usually use it on mah right foot when it gets cold, since mah rheumatism gets worse on that foot. This here is mah lighter. I ain't much of a smoker, but it's nice when you need a far. We ain't havin' no far here, though. Summon'll see the flame er smoke, for certain – that's a sure way to get found and lose our place. It ain't that cold anyhow, so we don't need no far."

"Here's mah hooch. Got half 'er bottle left. Been takin' it easy on the hooch terday – makin' it last. Yer'll be best to stay clear o my hooch. This ol' Red Dawg, I aim not to share." Ernest took a healthy swig, smiled and mouthed an audible, "Aah!" then screwed the translucent plastic cap back onto the bottle of clear, antiseptic-smelling liquid.

Sam was tired and began to doze off as Ernest continued his inventory. While this day, like several before it, had started in a haze of confusion and concern, his thoughts came more easily now with a full stomach. Though his his body still stung in spots from Ernest's strong back-hand, Sam did feel that Ernest could be his friend. He had orchestrated a meal and found a dry place to spend the night – both huge luxuries in this transient life Sam found himself living. It was certainly possible that Ernest was a threat, but Sam had nowhere else to go and was hopeful that Ernest could help find more food tomorrow. Sam opened his eyes again, paying some attention to his new friend's droning, as Ernest pulled a framed photograph from his pack.

"This here's mah son and daughter. They live with their mama, 'cause she kin take good care of 'em. I wasn't no good fer 'em, see. I couldn't never hold me a real job, and most of the jobs I had didn't pay so much either. So, they couldn't have no stuff that the other kids had. I also like the hooch, but it don't like me. It takes mah money and makes me mean. When I drank the hooch, I found myself hittin' their mom, my Shondra Lee. That ain't no good fer her or them kids. It ain't no good fer anybody. So I left 'em with their mother. But I still miss 'em a lot. I always liked to take 'em to the duck pond at the park. Them ducks would sure eat a loaf of bread awful quick, they would. And, them kids would giggle the whole time. I sure miss 'em, but I cain't go back 'cause I ain't no good fer 'em. Anyway, their mother would never let me at 'em anyway. She's a great mother thatta way, she is."

This night was the first good sleep that Sam could remember. While the noise of the late trains woke him a few times, the shelter and the blanket comforted him back to slumber quickly. The night was cold, but the concrete of the bridge seemed to insulate the pair, and Sam's coat provided excellent warmth. His stomach was full. He had hope that he may get a decent meal tomorrow. All in all, it was a great recipe for a good night's rest. The only interruption came in the early morning hours as Ernest began to toss and turn in his sleep.

"I'm sorry, Shondra Lee! Puhleez take mah back, puhleez! I'll stay away from that damned Red Dawg, yer'll see! I'm sorry, Shondra Lee!" Ernest wimpered on, but never truly came awake.

The next morning, Sam woke to the sound of Ernest whistling as he packed his bag. "Let's git up an go, Sam. We're a team now, and we have lots of *opportunities*!"

3. Homeless Again

Sam found the concrete pad beneath the Cincinnati Avenue bridge to be a wonderful dwelling for a number of weeks. It was secure and private, and provided excellent protection from the unpredictable Oklahoma spring weather. It was a great place for Sam and Ernest to meet and share the day's events after the occasions when they struck out on their own business. Because Ernest had invited him in to that home, Sam was quite confident that Ernest was a true friend and placed a good bit of trust in him. Ernest shared the location of the concrete pad with none of the other *rough sleepers* they encountered, and Sam kept the secret as well.

Ernest's foot continued to heal through the weeks, giving him the comfort and confidence to walk about the downtown area. In doing so, Ernest shared with Sam a good number of helpful hints for prosperous living on the street. These tricks had fed Sam's hunger many times, and had kept him out of several potentially dangerous situations. Sam was truly grateful for the kindness and compassion that Ernest had shown, and he always attempted to show his appreciation whenever he could.

Interestingly, there were two occasions since they set up beneath the bridge when a brown paper grocery bag had mysteriously appeared near the hole in the fence where they entered. The grocery bags both contained some bread and peanut butter. The second one also contained a box of eight Twinkies.

"I'm damned happy them do-gooders are leavin' us some chow. I ain't sure why they'd do somethin' like that, but I'm happy they do!" Ernest would say.

Sam and Ernest would share the food like this, as well as food they found in other ways. However, despite the close friendship forming between the pair, Ernest still liked to drink alone. Ernest was not interested in sharing his elixir, and Sam was happy to give Ernest some space when he needed it. Sam found that Ernest became mean and hateful when he had too many sips of the Red Dawg. In fact, were it not for Sam's quick reflexes, Ernest surely would have struck him with another rough backhand or another empty bottle during a fit of alcohol-induced rage.

On a sunny Saturday morning in May, Sam found Ernest beginning to reminisce about his wife and children. Despite his separation from his family and Ernest's insistence that they were better off without him, Ernest harbored volumes of remorse for staying away. He tortured himself by reliving happy moments that he knew were now beyond his reach, and followed those memories with laments about how they had continued living without him. Once fully enraged, Ernest would bawl and howl as he agonized over the separation he had created. Using those pains as a springboard, Ernest took on an unusually early *conversation* with his friend, the Red Dawg. The Red Dawg was his friend, his enemy, his crutch and his master of torture, all combined into a pint of clear liquid wrapped in a brown paper bag.

Ernest's psyche would descend to this cheerless state a few times each week. Sam thought of these episodes as Ernest's *sad times.* They might be brought on by seeing a family on the street or the discarded arm of a doll or teddy bear as he traveled the alleys. They might be brought on by simple boredom when Ernest's thoughts wandered to the places that depressed him. Sam didn't know exactly what things would cause the sad times – just that they happened and it was hard to be near Ernest when they did. Today, as he saw the sad times coming on, Sam determined that he would prefer not to witness the scene and so decided to head out for a stroll in the city.

Ernest's farewell to Sam was, as always, "Yer watch fer them damn cars, ya hear? They'll git ya befur you knows it and yer'll get yer a ride to nowhere. Jest watch yer step!"

Sam started west to visit the Kendall Whittier neighborhood. It was a vibrant place, and always had lots of interesting things going on. There, he found some children playing soccer in the street and was able to join in the fun until a watchful parent chased him away. From Kendall Whittier, he circled around to the university, which often had similar activities. It was quiet this day, so after exploring the campus and then window shopping in the eclectic shops of the Greenwood District, he found himself hungry and made the short trip to the trash Dumpsters behind the historical downtown hotels to find a light lunch. One of the many survival techniques Ernest had shown Sam was how the hotels consistently emptied their kitchen trash between the mid-day crowds and the evening crowds. Depending on what was on the lunch menu at the hotel restaurant, the kitchen trash would often provide relatively fresh morsels for those who took the initiative to raid the bins. In preparation to stake his claim, Sam took a sheltered position across the alley from a favorite bin. He positioned himself between a gas meter and an air conditioning unit, and was not visible to the half-dozen workers who carried out two large bags each from the kitchen. However, he could see three other *rough sleepers* who he'd be competing with for the best morsels. He calculated that if he could see three, then there were probably an additional three he could not see who would also appear when the workers were finished. As usual, he would have to rely on his cunning and exceptional foot speed to get the best meal.

To target his approach, Sam carefully observed each of the shiny black plastic bags as workers tossed them into the Dumpsters. He dismissed the lighter bags, as they were likely breads and salads – edible, but not particularly satisfying. On the other hand, his experience told him that the heavier bags likely contained the leftover meats or vegetables. To further narrow the field, Sam also looked for the shapes of bones pressing through the sides of the bags. Sam's favorite dish of hotel restaurant leftovers was the roasted chicken. For reasons he did not comprehend, those bones always seemed to have ample meat remaining. He was skilled at removing those leftovers from the bones, and they felt amazingly warm and comfortable in his stomach. The actual temperature of the garbage was not a factor. Sam eyed the most desirable of the bags, based on his semi-scientific criteria, and saw two good targets thrown into the bin nearest him. He declared in his mind that the best of those bags would be his, and was determined to not be denied.

The workers dragged their heavy loads into the alley, heaving the garbage onto other black bags that had collected in the Dumpsters since the trash truck had last visited. When all the bags were securely deposited, they slammed the heavy lids closed with a metallic clang that hurt Sam's ears. Finally, the workers settled in for an impromptu *siesta* and passed a match around as they each lit a cigarette and began to leisurely inhale the smelly poison from the white sticks. The *rough sleepers*, with their mouths watering in anticipation of the meal, waited impatiently in their positions for the workers to finish their break. When the last of the cigarettes was burned down sufficiently, the workers flicked the still-glowing butts into the alley with a simple motion of their thumb and forefinger, and disappeared into the back of the hotel. When the heavy metal door slammed shut, the *rough sleepers* jumped into action.

Sam knew that he was fast enough to be at his target Dumpster before any of the others. However, he was wise enough to let the young man beside him break ahead of him on the way to the closest one. Per Sam's plan, the young man was delayed as he lifted the heavy lid. While he wrestled to secure it, Sam jumped past him, dove up into the bin, and quickly located his chosen black bags. He carefully sniffed at the opening of each, and chose between the three based on the scent of chicken and stuffing, deftly tearing the bag open and focusing on the meal of the afternoon. By the time the young man had secured the lid, Sam had eaten the remnants of a broiled chicken, a large portion of stuffing, and then grabbed another chicken portion to eat on the way back home. He jumped out from the Dumpster and sprinted down the alley as the young man who opened the lid for him shouted some colorful obscenities in Sam's wake. Sam was thankful for his natural speed and agility, and made no apologies for it. In situations like this, his gifts help provide a warm and tasty meal. There was no substitute for speed in nature, and no substitute for speed on the street.

Sam stopped by the Bartlett Square fountain to finish his chicken, leaving the nearly-clean bones behind as a monument to his conquest. As he bent down to take a sip from the fountain, he noticed the cloudy sky in the reflection from the water. After drinking his fill, Sam studied the clouds and knew he needed to hurry back to the concrete pad beneath the bridge if he didn't want to be soaked with the rain. He gauged that he had about six blocks to travel. It wasn't a particularly long distance, but it wasn't insignificant either. Sam jogged two blocks to the east, then turned north on Cincinnati Avenue as the sky opened with a flash and a loud clap of thunder. He stepped into a full sprint as he pushed for the bridge, feeling the heavy rain drops striking, then soaking through his coat and beginning to give him a chill. While this certainly wasn't the first time Sam had been caught in the open during a thunderstorm, the winds were particularly brutal on this day, forcing the water down at an angle nearly horizontal to the ground. The rain began to get heavier and heavier, and it stung his face as he ran. Sam found his way to the hole in the chain-link fence, darted through, then curved beneath the bridge to catch his breath.

As he filled his lungs, Sam felt a hand slap down on his shoulder.

"I'm glad to see yer back. Yer sure don't want ter git caught in that ol' storm terday!"

Sam marveled at the sound of the rain mixed with bursts of thunder, watching the sideways rain turn to white pellets of ice. The hail started at about the size of un-popped popcorn seeds, but quickly grew to the size of olives, then to the size of tater-tots. Sam began to realize how close he had come to being bruised and pummeled by Mother Nature's violence. The air around him became noticeably colder as the ice accumulated, and the blanket of hail melted into a soup of ice balls with the steady rain mixed in. Hail that fell on the bridge above was washed over the edge by the rushing water, adding to the mix surrounding the pair.

As usual, Ernest verbalized the feeling, "Hot damn, Sam! Yer'd have been beat to kingdom come if yer'd stayed out there much longer. I's glad yer decided to come back when yer did. I heard of a feller over yonder by the river that got hisself caught in th' open in a damned hailstorm. It beat pop knots across his head an' shoulders that lasted near a month!"

"Damn, that hurts!" Sam and Ernest heard a strange voice over the sound of the hail. "Where the hell'd you go, you speedy son of a bitch!"

Sam listened to the sound of someone pressing through the hole in the chain link, then saw a dark shape stumble from the rain and hail into the shelter beneath the bridge. A moment earlier, Sam had enjoyed the scent of the rain. He had taken notice of how the rain had brought the smell of dust down from the sky as it cleaned and cooled the air simultaneously. Yet now, the smell of this stranger simply took Sam's breath away. It wasn't the smell of rancid food, nor the natural musk of a man many days from his last bath. It was painful to Sam's nose. The pungent stench was acidic and toxic and frightful.

"I'm sure glad I seen you dart through that hole in the fence – that bright yellow coat of yours makes it easier to see where you're headed," the stranger went on. "Damn! Them hail are gettin' bigger and bigger. I'd have been beat up for sure if I didn't get under here. Just look at that!" The stranger shook his head as he watched the hail come down, slowing turning the brown muddy soil and green patches of spring weeds growing around the railroad tracks to a white glaze that looked almost like snow cover. "I watched you eating that chicken by the fountain and was following you to see if I could find some too. Damn, it looked good. Then, it started raining on us and you made a break for it. You sure are a fast som'bitch. I was keeping up 'til you started that sprint. Lucky I saw where you turned. Damn, I sure don't like that hail coming down." The stranger shook some of the water from his worn brown denim jacket and torn blue jeans. "I'm completely soaked. Wow!" He gazed around the shelter beneath the bridge. "This looks like a good spot to put down for a while." He smiled a wide grin, displaying two rows of yellow teeth that appeared to be whittled down to nubs. "I'll bet I can get a friend to give me a fix or two for settin' 'em up in here. What a great place to get hooked up!" He looked back at Ernest and Sam. "Hi! I'm Chris," the stranger said, offering a hand for Ernest to shake.

Ernest ignored the gesture. "This here's our place. Yer can stay 'til the hail stops, then yer need to git on yer way where yer belong. I kin see whut that meth smokin' has done ter ya. Yer ain't got no teeth left and yer thin as a rail. I kin smell it too. Yer and your buddies ain't gonna screw this here place up fer us."

Sam could see that Chris was legitimately surprised by the cool reception he received from Ernest. Nonetheless, Chris was not deterred.

"You aren't too friendly, are you? We all have our issues, old man. That pink nose of yours tells me you've been nipping on something yourself. It don't seem to me that you have room to judge my kind of recreation when you have your own kind of recreation." Sam thought there was actually a bit of logic to the junkie's statement. "Oh, say what you want. That's okay. I'm happy enough to have found this place. I like it, and my friends will too! It will be a great place to smoke up!"

"Yer don't have no business here after this rain," Ernest took a threatening step forward with Sam by his side. Chris knew he was no match for Ernest and Sam, and wisely chose not to engage in this particular battle.

"Looks like I don't have no choice today. But, this place is too good to keep to yourselves. That's plumb selfish! Since you're not sharing now, I'll not be sharing when I bring a few friends back with me to move in." Chris, having made his intentions very clear, took a step toward the edge of the concrete slab. He sat down facing the interior of the shelter, leaned back and stretched, "I'll take off when that weather settles down, but for now, I'm going to take a nice hit and size up my new living room."

Chris flashed another yellow-toothed grin with his sparsely populated mouth, dug a crinkled plastic sandwich bag from his soaked pocket, and assembled his apparatus to partake of his meth. While he appeared to take his time, Sam noticed the man's hands shake with anticipation as he worked. Chris used a small plastic cigarette lighter to ignite the chemical, then took a deep draw from the pipe. He held the fumes in his lungs, closed his eyes and slowly exhaled, then lay back to enjoy whatever it was he found pleasurable in destroying his body. The fumes from the pipe drifted through the air, and Sam now understood the poison smell that Chris had brought into the shelter. He saw Ernest turn up his nose as well, and the pair found a sheltered place as far from Chris as they could.

"Well, I s'pose the gig's over here," Ernest spoke softly. "We could take 'im now, but 'e'll be back with more of them meth heads and ruin it. It's time fer us to find another place ter stay. Let's wait this storm out and we'll head out to find sompn else in the mornin'."

Sam felt sad and remorseful, and Ernest could see it in his eyes.

"Don't yer worry none. It coulda happened to either of us. I know yer was runnin to get out of the storm. Who'd've thunk summon was follerin yer. Don't yer worry. We'll find us sompn else right quick."

Sam felt better about the situation. Ernest always had ideas on where to go and what to do, and Sam was confident that Ernest would come through again.

"I'll do some thinkin' here fur a bit, and we'll go house huntin' when I git a list in mah head. There's plenty o' real estate in this town. We'll just need ter choose wisely again." Ernest was always the optimist.

Later that afternoon, when the rain subsided and the sun broke through the clouds, Chris departed as promised. He pointedly reminded Ernest and Sam of his intentions to return. "I'll be seeing you two real soon. I hope you clean the place up to get ready for some company. The high's so much better when you have a good place to enjoy it. I'll be back right soon to see my new living room again. Maybe I'll even let you stick around for a day 'er two – only as long as you clean up after us and keep the place tidy," he jeered.

Sam took a close look at Chris as he smiled and made his threats. Sam could tell that Chris was once a formidable man – tall and stout. But his age had accumulated more rapidly than his years, partly from his time living on the street, but more from the smelly pipe he worshiped. His demon left a gaunt shell of what could have been an impressive body, teeth rotting away with each hit of the meth. Chris continued his rant and progressed through a litany of obscene gestures toward Sam and Ernest until he had exited through the hole in the chain link fence and was out of sight.

Sam was happy to have Chris gone, but agreed with Ernest that Chris would make good on his promise to return with more of his smelly crew, easily outnumbering them. Recalling his early days on the street, Sam didn't look forward to the exhaustion and disorientation he experienced when he had no place to peacefully rest. Ernest sensed the concern in Sam's eyes and worked to put him at ease.

"We'll be fine here ternight. We'll just need to listen for the chain link to rattle and be ready to run if we need ter. We'll gather our stuff so we can make a quick exit. T'morrow, we'll find a new spot. Maybe even better. Probly even better. I know lots of good places and lots of good people. We'll find a place that suits us jest fine."

Sam was dubious – it was hard to envision a home better than this concrete pad. However, Ernest had come through last time, and Sam would trust him to come through again.

"T'morrow, we'll visit the churches and gather up some workin' captal, then we'll find us a new spot ter rest our heads," Ernest reiterated. "I'm packin up our stuff, then let's get us a good night's sleep before we moves on." And, with that, the pair prepared to leave the comfort of the concrete pad beneath the Cincinnati Avenue bridge and settled in for the last night's rest.

4. Invitation

The following morning was the start of a glorious Oklahoma May Sunday, and Ernest had intentions to make the rounds through the churches. Ernest had a process for gathering up cash money to obtain life's necessities. Sometimes Sam would go on the rounds with Ernest, sometimes not. On this day Sam had nowhere else to be and chose to come along to watch Ernest operate in his element.

"Well, sir, mah name's Ernest and this is mah friend, Sam. Mah car is broke down, outta gas, over yonder there on the Broken Arrow Expressway. Mah wife, Shondra Lee and mah kids is waitin for me. I hated to leave 'em on the highway like that, but I thought it was safer than havin' them kids walking beside the road. So, I just came down this way to git some gas, but I don't have enough cash for gas money. Mah car gits good miles on a gallon o gas, so I thank I kin get to Bartlesville on about five dollars. Kin you spare a little sompn for a feller tryin to get his fam'ly home?"

Ernest had the pitch down pat, and he could tune it just so to pull the heart strings of his audience of the moment. This particular gentleman, trying to peacefully depart from the Sunday morning service at the Downtown Episcopal Church, had smartly marched his two young boys and wife into their car while he politely listened to Ernest and looked for a place to turn him down.

"I don't think I have much cash with me," he weakly objected as he tried to enter his car.

"Well, sir, every little bit would help out here. Do yer see any change on the floor of yer car? We'll help yer look if yer think yer might. As a daddy, ah'd just like ter git mah family home, ya know?" It was an excellent move to allow the man to identify with Ernest's faux situation.

"No, no. It looks like my wife found something for you," he replied as she handed the man a couple of dollars that he passed over to Ernest and quickly sat down in the driver's seat.

"Thank yer so much. Mah wife and kids will be so happy to be home." Ernest concluded the deal as the gentleman quickly sped off in his sedan, the boys' noses pressed to the rear windows watching Ernest and Sam as they went.

"Not a bad mornin' fer us, eh partner?" Ernest asked rhetorically, "Looks like we've cleared eighteen dollars and sixty-eight cents. That ain't bad at all! We got enough for a little hooch and a little chow already. Let's see if we can git one er two from the Baptists before we calls it a day."

Ernest and Sam had worked their way across most all the downtown church parking lots. Ernest had studied the church service times and had plotted a course from the Methodists to the Presbyterians to the Lutherans to the Episcopals, so that they could weave across downtown just as the congregations were departing for a warm, family lunch. The Baptists were always last because their services seemed to run longer than any of the others. Ernest thought the Baptists must be smarter than the rest because they seemed to get more religion for their money than any of the other denominations.

Sam had heard Ernest admit it: The *car with family in it out of gas* pitch was certainly a bit deceitful compared with traditional panhandling, or *handlin'* as Ernest called it. However, deceit or not, it was especially effective in church parking lots on Sunday. The psychology of the reasons for the pitch's effectiveness would make an exceptional case study for an MBA student studying marketing. The "customers," as Ernest liked to call them, were fresh out of a church service that likely underscored the righteousness of helping a fellow man. Good target customers were parents, and the parents didn't want their children exposed to creatures of the street like Ernest and Sam. Further, the children were normally hungry and restless after an hour and half of listening to adult-targeted religious dogma and liturgy. All in all, the parents wanted to get on their way as quickly as possible without sinning against Ernest and Sam. Understandably, the pitch played on a customer's sense of altruism and his selfishness at the same time. As a result, a contribution of some amount was likely from anyone properly approached. It didn't have to be anything substantial; just some pocket change would do. Even those small amounts would add up over the course of the day.

Sam made his way to the north side of the Baptist church parking lot and sat down on the sidewalk with Ernest to contemplate their housing situation while they waited for the service to let out.

"It's great to have some dinero for chow, but we'd best find ourselves a new sleepin' spot right soon," Ernest mused. "I'm feelin' some rain comin' in my rheumatism foot. That foots' better'n an OU meteorology d'gree, ahl say. I can predict it better'n them TV forecasters."

43

Sam heard the pianist begin the postlude music inside the church, a classical piece for which he had little appreciation. He saw the carved wooden doors open, and families begin to stream through on their way back to their cars. The volume of people started pretty light, but when the preacher made his appearance outside the door, the numbers quickly increased, each adult congregant warmly shaking the preachers hand as they passed by him.

Sam watched Ernest study the families as they squinted in the sunlight and smiled at each other after their Sunday spiritual recharge. He was obviously looking for the most likely volunteer to donate to a fellow down on his luck. "Let's get a customer or two here, then we'll head on down the road to see what livin' space is available. A change er scene-ry will do us both right. We'll find us sompn good over yonder there. I knows several places we can check. Let's start with that'n headed for the blue van. They'll want to get them kids out'er here before I do much talkin' to 'em. They'll be good customers, I can jest feel it."

Sam was truly impressed as the blue van family blushed and handed over two dollars in bills plus some coins they found in their pockets. He watched Ernest approach two other similar families, with similar results, before deciding they were pressing their luck and should move along. While there was nothing officially illegal about deceiving these good people out of their money using the *car with family in it out of gas* pitch, the local police and leaders of the churches found it bad for business and strongly discouraged *rough sleepers* from pursuing such activities. The best bet for Sam and Ernest was to get a reasonable take and move ahead before someone pressed back.

"We scored us more'n twenty-four dollars this mornin'! I'm feeling the need for some Red Dawg, so les make a stop at the Liquor Mart for a quick stock up. Should cost us about ten of them hard-earned dollars."

The pair proceeded down Detroit Avenue to the Liquor Mart on Eleventh Street. The Liquor Mart was one of the few standalone businesses remaining in the southern part of downtown. All the other small buildings that were built in the early part of the twentieth century had since been torn down to make way for either high-rise office buildings, attached storefront businesses, or vast parking lots. The windows and glass front door were covered with black bars on the outside and posters of beer and liquor advertisements on the inside, effectively blocking the view into the store. The building sat back from the street, allowing enough room for a small gravel-covered parking lot. No lines were painted on the lot to direct the parking, so depending on how the patrons aligned their cars, the lot could hold between two and five vehicles. Sam inspected the gravel beneath his feet as he crossed the lot with Ernest, finding green and brown bits of broken glass mixed in with the dust and rock covering. There were no cars in the lot at this time, which struck the pair as unusual until Ernest noticed the "Closed" sign on the front door.

"Damn Oklahoma liquor laws. I shoulda knowed that terday's Sunday and the Liquor Mart has ter be closed. Them same damned Baptists and Lutherans who gave to our cause terday are the same ones who close the damned Liquor Mart on Sundays. Them an' the pol'ticians. Bastards, all of 'em! How's a feller s'posed ter get a shot o' hooch?" Ernest swore at the door, the sky, Sam and the empty gravel parking lot. The rant was a good way for Ernest to vent, but it didn't change the "Closed" sign on the door.

Sam heard a new set of footsteps crunching across the gravel parking lot.

"I don't have any Red Dawg, but I know I got something you need, there fella," offered the new voice. Ernest grinned as Sam sized up the woman. She was shorter than Ernest but taller than Sam. She was stout, and Sam gauged that while she limped as she walked, she could move quickly if she needed to do so. Like most street residents, or *rough sleepers*, she wore a tattered coat, even in the warmth of May, and walked with a bit of a tired shuffle. All in all, Sam did not see that she presented an immediate threat to Ernest or himself and so he relaxed as she approached.

"Rosine!" Ernest waved as he returned the greeting. "Are ya still sellin' yerself out, you ol' bat?"

"Hell, no, Ernest! I got roughed up a few months back, so I don't look quite so inviting. Besides, I'm gettin' old and no one'l have me anymore." She stopped as she reached Sam and Ernest. "Now, I'm havin' to make an *honest* livin' like the rest of you!"

"Well, I hate ter hear that. I can see you're lookin' a little rough terday, but I's sure there's lots of days when yer'll be lookin' right d'sirable. Ah, hell, I don't have no money for yer anyhow."

"You're still full of shit, Ernest," Rosine keenly observed, "If you don't have any money, then what are you doing complaining to God 'n everyone about the Oklahoma liquor laws in front of this here Liquor Mart on a pretty Sunday afternoon? I'll wager that you got the dough, but couldn't make it happen if you needed to!"

Rosine beamed a toothy grin at Ernest, knowing that she had hit the truth and a nerve as well, trying to give him an opportunity to salvage a little pride.

"Honey," he retorted, "a man's got ter have his priorities straight, and I guess yer can see 'em here. Today's def'nitely a day where I'll take a shot 'o hooch over yer, for shor!" Ernest felt a little air puffing back into his ego.

As Ernest's grin came back across his blushed face, a grey minivan pulled into the parking lot and came to a stop with the driver's side near the group. As the tinted window came down, Ernest looked to the driver to inform him, "Save yer time, feller. The Baptists and damned Oklahoma legislature has closed this store fer the day! No hooch fer us honest citizens t'day!"

The opening window revealed the soft white face of a "customer" from earlier in the day. "So, I see that this must be your wife, and him with the dirty yellow coat must be your kid that was waiting by the side of the road! I'm so glad to see that you're using that money to get home to Bartlesville! You're a lying sack of shit!"

The window raised back up as quickly as it was lowered down and the back of the van slipped dangerously close to the trio as its tires spewed small pieces of gravel from the parking lot.

"Damn! That was close!" breathed Ernest, believing he had a near-death experience.

"Another satisfied customer, huh?" Rosine chuckled. "I guess you stick to the tried and true, don't cha? I guess you gotta go with what works! I bet the reverend wouldn't be pleased with that ol boy's profanity, though!"

"Aw, we all got it in us. Yer cain't blame a feller for gettin' riled up over bein had," Ernest observed. "So, what cha been doin' lately? I haven't seen yer since the fall when we were handlin' the car wash on Fifteenth Street. I thought maybe yer had moved on. 'Specially when the weather got cold. Traffic in that car wash goes to nuthin' when it gits cold, yer know. Ain't no handlin' ter be done. Where'd yer settle?"

"Me and a couple others set up camp near the river – we staked a nice spot by the Twenty Third Street Bridge. We settled in for the winter and just decided to stay. We've been stayin' quiet to keep the po-lice, druggies and gang-bangers out. So far, so good."

"Sam, here, and me jest left a pretty good spot, but it got taken by some meth smokers and we couldn't stand the smell, so we're a bit between places. Der ya spose we could wait out a storm er two with yer while we're gettin' our feet under us?" Sam noticed that Ernest was always looking for an opportunity. "I'm sure you'd be willin' to help a feller who's down on his luck," Ernest grinned.

"I think an offering of some chow would work wonders for a night or two with us," Rosine suggested. "But understand that the others will certainly worry about keeping the place quiet. If you give us away, you know there'll be hell to pay. Right? You gotta know that we have an enforcer that you won't want to mess with."

"Surely," Ernest said in agreement. "We'll not breathe a word to no one." Sam smiled inside, knowing that he would have a place to sleep for the night. Sam also knew that were it not for the Oklahoma liquor laws, the Liquor Mart would be open and their money would have been spent on Red Dawg instead of some food supplies to pay the rent for the night. He was torn between his happiness to have a place to stay and the discomfort he knew Ernest would feel. Sam was happier when Ernest was happier, but today, when the sad time came, Ernest would have to face his feelings without the help of his friend, the Red Dawg. Sam concluded that might not be all bad. Maybe Ernest's sad time would pass easier without the crutch.

"Lead the way, Honey!" cackled Ernest. "We'll foller yer."

"OK. We'll make a trip to the Grocery Stop on the way so you can do a little stocking up."

Sam and Ernest followed Rosine west along Eleventh Street toward the river on their way to the Grocery Stop. The old store was just outside downtown in a building that looked much like the Liquor Mart. The glass was the same, the black bars on the windows were the same, but the advertisements on the glass were for mayonnaise and pickles and soda pop instead of beer and liquor. The most important difference was that the Grocery Stop was open on this Sunday afternoon.

The trio could see that the small store was empty of customers as they walked in the door. A clerk was stationed behind a counter near the front. He maintained a stubble-farm on his face nearly as rough as Ernest's, and balanced the nub of a mostly-smoked Marlboro in the corner of his mouth. His plastic name tag read "Heinrich." Heinrich was likely not the first to enjoy a Marlboro at the counter. Years of the toxic smoke had permanently stained the walls and, along with the accompanying old-smoke odor, created the dingy ambience of an old nightclub. Nonetheless, the clerk's Marlboro added fresh stench to the small store, annoying Sam almost as much as the meth smoke that Chris had blown in his face the day before. Heinrich had no idea that anyone would be bothered by his habit, and wouldn't have cared had he known. His fingernails needed to be trimmed and they carried splotchy deposits of dirt and grease on the underside. Like his current customers, personal hygiene was not at the top of the clerk's priority list.

Heinrich was engrossed in the process of scratching the yellowish-gold wax covering from his lottery ticket using the edge of a quarter. The gold wax peeled away from the paper and fell to the floor as he scraped the coin back and forth across the ticket. After a dozen or so scrapes, he took a drag on his cigarette, pursed his lips and exhaled smoke to blow the remaining wax crumbs from the paper.

"Damn!" he muttered under his breath, indicating that he had donated yet another dollar to the Oklahoma Lottery. Heinrich placed the used ticket on a stack beside the cash register. He appeared to be approaching five inches of losing lottery tickets, demonstrating the lottery's reputation as a state tax aimed at citizens with poor math skills

Sufficiently disgusted with his loss, the clerk looked up to see the patrons and immediately frowned at them.

"Hey! What are you doing in here? Do you have any money? Let me see your money or I will call the police now!"

The clerk had obviously dealt with *rough sleepers* in the past and was comfortable being assertive, even aggressive, to avoid watching his inventory walk out the door under the coats and in the stomachs of the hungry and desperate homeless population who frequented his store.

Ernest spoke up, "Settle down, son! We're legit! Don't we look legit ter you?"

"No, you do not! Let me see your money or I will call the police now!"

Ernest waved the wad of bills he had collected earlier in the day for the clerk to see. Still not convinced of the trio's true motivations in the store, the clerk ordered, "OK – just one of you. The other two – you without the money! You must wait outside!"

Sam was reluctant to leave Ernest and stayed close, eyeing the angry clerk and sizing him up. Heinrich, showing that he was not one to be taken lightly, picked up the telephone and began dialing. Only then did Rosine push Sam by the shoulder, breaking his stare and moving him back out through the door.

Once outside, Rosine sat down on the curb and lit up a Marlboro of her own. Sam, however, was uncomfortable with Ernest being in the store alone with the foul clerk. Sam paced along the sidewalk, going from the front door past the newspaper machine, past the ice machine to the pay phone, then turning around going back to the front door and repeating the cycle. He could see inside between the signs hung on the windows, and was relieved each time he caught a glimpse of Ernest in an aisle picking out food for their offering.

"Don't cha worry, there Sam," Rosine consoled, "he'll be out right quick. Say, I sure do like that yella coat of yours. Ya want to hang on to that and take care of it – it'll do you some good in the cold weather." She took a deep drag on her cigarette. "I wish I had something that looked like that. I'll have to keep my eyes open for one, don't you think?"

Ernest made his way back to the counter, paid for his selections, and returned to the sidewalk without incident.

Sam was immediately relieved and rushed over to evaluate Ernest's shopping. He had white bread, sliced bologna, cheese puffs and popcorn covered in artificial butter. All would most certainly be a hit for their hosts this evening. Rosine smiled her approval as well.

The group started toward Denver Avenue which would lead down to the river trail. When the slope of the hill took the Grocery Stop from their line of sight, Ernest stopped and handed the bag of food to Rosine.

"Could yer hold this for jist a minute?" he asked, and began pulling additional goodies from his pockets and the linings of his coat. He dropped an additional six chocolate bars into the bag, along with another package of bologna, some sliced provolone cheese and five aluminum cans of beer. Ernest popped the top on the sixth beer and took a long draw. "It ain't Red Dawg, but it'll do fer a Sunday! Take one from the bag if yer want!" Rosine obliged him. Ernest tossed a final plastic package of sliced roast beef to Sam, who downed the tasty meat on the spot. Sam would go to war for Ernest; Ernest was always thinking of him and was a great friend.

5. The Clearing

After enjoying the Sunday afternoon snack, the group made their way down Denver Avenue to Riverside Drive, a scenic boulevard that followed the Arkansas River from downtown all the way out to the suburbs. They turned onto a narrow, paved trail that paralleled the river through the city at least ten miles in each direction. The smooth asphalt trail was the non-automobile artery of the city, meandering through the narrow swath of parkland that separated Riverside Drive from the river itself. The trail attracted runners, bikers and skaters from all over the city, and on a sunny Sunday afternoon was busier than usual. Sam and Ernest both knew that Rosine's group must be well-hidden to avoid detection by the thousands of people who visited the park each weekend. The settlement had to be far enough away from the trail that a child wandering through the woods would not accidentally stumble upon them. Yet, how far could it be? The trail was here, and the river was only twenty feet away.

Rosine noticed Ernest and Sam's confusion and counseled, "Don't worry. We have a little ways to go. As we approach the bridge, the trail sneaks away from the main part of the river. We'll dart off around that next bend. You two watch your backs – we don't want someone to see us leave the trail."

They continued on, and Sam could see a bridge in the distance. The trail began to veer away from the river as Rosine indicated it would, and the brush began to grow thicker and large oak and maple trees added to the barrier between the trail and the river.

"We'll head off behind that ol' bench 'round the next corner. Just follow me. Try not to break t'many branches as we pass through 'cause them trees and brush are our camouflage," warned Rosine. "The fellers are goin' to be sore enough at me for bringin' you here in the first place. If y'all beat a public path to our home, they'll have my hide and yours too!"

They came upon the park bench where the trail widened and curved directly in front of them. It was a heavy metal structure covered in a thick, dark green plastic coating, set into the ground beside the path with concrete. The earth around the jagged concrete footings, which was worn bare from constant foot traffic, had eroded, exposing an inch or two of the concrete above the ground. The bench had evidently been in place for a long time, as the plastic coating had become dull from oxidation where the sun hit the bench. To add to the ambiance of the setting, many lovers had carved their initials into the plastic coating on the flat parts of the back and seat, allowing a brownish rust to form and bubble up from the metal frame below.

"That ain't as r'mantic as carvin' in a tree trunk, but I guess it got the job done," observed Ernest as they passed.

"Whut the hell do you know about romance?" Rosine countered, "Just follow me, Casanova."

"I'll bet yer've said that a few times before," Ernest jeered, stumbling as he followed Rosine through the reeds and tall weeds.

"Damn, Ernest!" Rosine scolded Ernest to change the subject as she observed the damage to the foliage in his wake. "You walk like an elephant! You're leaving a trail of broken branches and squashed grass. Shit. The boys are gonna have our hides. At least your friend Sam knows how to walk softly in the forest. Way to go, son!"

Another fifty feet through the tall grass and brush brought the group into a flat clearing. It was a very comfortable place, and Sam understood why Rosine and her friends would want to keep it secret from others in the community. Sam and Ernest turned to look behind them, and saw only a wall of tall grass and brush ambling up the higher part of the river bank. The Twenty Third Street Bridge bordered the clearing to the south, with large concrete pilings decorating that end of the clearing. To the west, the waters of the Arkansas River swiftly carried snowmelt from Colorado as well as the spring rains of Kansas and western Oklahoma down toward the Gulf of Mexico. Despite the heavy flow, the clearing was easily twenty feet above the waterline, with a gentle slope down that could almost function as a beach or boat ramp. There was no view of the people on the jogging trail well above them. Sam listened carefully, and could barely make out the sound of traffic and other activity above.

The clearing allowed the sunshine in, but also provided excellent privacy. The only places with any view of the clearing would be the river itself, which rarely had boat traffic of any kind, or from above on the bridge. The inhabitants had wisely positioned their three tattered tents at the edge of the clearing directly below the bridge. The center tent, by far the largest, was facing away from them. It was a dark green canvas affair, tall enough for most adults to stand in, propped up with three metal poles and a relatively straight tree branch substituting for the fourth. The smaller, octagonal dome tents were staked down on either side of the large green one and slightly behind it. The blue octagonal tent was positioned to the left and the brown one to the right of the big green tent. The entry doors to all three tents faced each other, with what appeared to be a gathering area between them. The layout was roughly an isosceles triangle formed by the tents. There was enough room to walk between, but they were close enough together to share a number of grounding stakes. A line of twine was suspended between the big green tent and the brown dome, sagging a bit from some wet clothing hung from it.

"That's our place!" Rosine stated with pride. "We all have a tent, and we call the spot in the middle our courtyard, 'cause it's a great place for us to meet and talk."

Sam surveyed the location and silently declared it to be clever. The location eliminated the possibility that someone in a car would notice the tents from the bridge. Further, for a pedestrian to notice the cloister, he would be required to stop and look straight down with his head hung over the edge of the bridge, which was very unlikely. It was completely invisible from the main part of the river trail. In his world, privacy meant security, and this location provided some good security.

Rosine continued toward the triangle of tents. As she approached, a younger man, immensely broad and tall with sandy blond hair and a scruffy beard of matching color, crawled from the brown tent. He stood, scowled, and glowered down over Sam and Ernest.

"Rosine! What the hell do you think you're doing! How could you bring these two out here? You know the rules! Damn! What are you thinking?" he berated her, stomping over stakes and tie-downs as he walked toward the trio.

"C'mon, Gerald! This here's Ernest! You remember him from..."

Gerald held his palm up toward Rosine and stepped toward Ernest. Gerald's scowl reversed into a broad grin as he stood close to Ernest.

"I do remember Ernest," he said, "I do remember." And with a single motion, Gerald's had balled into a fist and came down smartly across Ernest's cheek and nose, knocking him flat on his back. "You dirty bastard! You ratted me out when I lived at the University! I had a warm place to sleep, reasonable meals, and access to the library, and you blew that for me! You need to pick yourself up and march your way out of here, before I tear your arms off your shoulders!"

Sam had let his guard down as Gerald cracked his initial grin, but was now on full alert and quickly placed himself between the two men, back to Ernest and chest to Gerald. Gerald saw the fire in Sam's eyes and knew that he could take the scuffle no further, despite his obvious desire to add bruises to the stunned Ernest.

"Okay, okay. I'm done for now. Ernest, you need to call your friend off. You both just need to turn around, go back, and forget you ever saw this place."

Ernest was still too stunned to answer, but Rosine jumped into the conversation. "But Gerald, wait! They brought some great dinner! Ya didn't think I'd just bring 'em here with nuthin' in hand, did ya? Can't they stay a night or two? I don't know what he did to you, but I've known Ernest for a long while, and he ain't never done me wrong!"

"I don't trust him none," Gerald grumbled. "That Ernest, he ratted me outta my home at the University. I went from a comfy, quiet place to living back on the street – just because Ernest wanted to pee in private! Damn, Ernest, why couldn't ya have just found a tree like anybody else with some common sense?"

Ernest was gathering his wits and couldn't help but begin to grin at the memory, which served to incense Gerald.

"Dammit, Ernest, it just ain't funny! That must've been in February, and it was damned cold wanderin' around after I was evicted! You're a bastard!"

"Will you two tell me what happened here," Rosine demanded. "I don't understand what you're grumbling about and what, *Ernest*, you're grinning about!"

"Well, Rosine, honey," Ernest stammered while holding back a chuckle and wincing at the pain of the shiner forming on his cheek, "A while back – must 'er been wintertime from what grumbly Gerry there says – I was new ter sleepin' *rough*, and wuz 'handling on 'Leventh street near the college. After I had made me some pocket change, I finished me a bottle of the Red Dawg and was wandering mah way across the grounds. As yer might expect, the Red Dawg caused a little pressure down south thar, and I felt me an urge to take a whiz. I didn't think it too proper to just let 'er loose on the grounds, an there wasn't no way they'd let a *rough sleeper* like me inside one of them nice buildings fer a urinal. But, while I was wanderin, I saw there was a port-a-john laid sideways between a great big evergreen bush and the Humanities building. It was a greenish color and wedged right up thar between that bush and that building – real hidden, like. Sommun would have to walk right up on 'er to see 'er, so I figgered the campus police jest hadn't noticed 'er after one of them kids had brought 'er back after a night 'o dancin' with the Red Dawg. So, I figgered ah'd jest do everone a favor. Ah'd jest stand that ol' port-a-john up, take a whiz in 'er and then leave 'er up so sommun would see 'er and take 'er where she belonged."

"Doing everyone a favor, hmff!" Gerald interjected. "Thanks a million!"

"Well," Ernest continued, "as I stood 'er up, I noticed that she didn't slosh so much, so I figured it wouldn't be too messy in thar even with 'er having rested on 'er side. When I opened the door, it was plenty clean, shore enough and I really didn't pay no attention to the pillers and blankets that was on the floor. I just stepped in and did mah bizness like any civilized feller would."

Ernest red face burst into a barrage of chuckles as he couldn't hold his laughter any longer, again furthering Gerald's anger.

"As I finished my bizness thar, summon jest about pounded through the door and skeered mah to death. Ol' Gerry here was crowin' about how I'd peed in his house and messed it all up! I didn't know what to think – hell, it was a port-a-john! What wuz I s'posed to do in 'er?"

"You're supposed to leave folks stuff alone, well enough! When you saw the dry bottom, the blanket and the pillows, you should have known that it wasn't *just* a port-a-john! You're a stupid old fart!"

Ernest was now doubled over in pain from laughter, having recovered from Gerald's blow, exultantly reliving the port-a-john scene and enjoying the retelling of it at least as much.

"The best part, 'o course," Ernest blurted between cackles, "was that I came right out ter have ol' Gerry here go on a rant! He tore mah up one side and down th' other 'til a crowd 'o them college kids gathered 'round and finally the campus police. Sure enough, you know them police boys ain't gonna put up with a couple of us *rough sleepers* arguin', much less keeping a port-a-john right thar on the side 'o that building. But yer know, Gerry, if yer would've jest kept your trap quiet and we'd have jest set 'er back down, yer'd probly still be livin' there!"

"Maybe so, but it took me a month to get the piss smell out of that plastic can the first time, and you just freshened it up for me. I still can't believe you did that! You're a dirty bastard!"

"Gerry, son, all I kin do now is tell yer that ah'm sorry. I just needed ter take a whiz! Yer can't fault a man fer that, can yer?"

Rosine was visibly amused by the recounting of Ernest's port-a-john blunder. Most *rough sleepers*, she thought, certainly would have recognized it as someone's home. But not Ernest, and definitely not Ernest after a bottle of Red Dawg.

"Gerald, let's leave that in the past." Rosine kept the amusement from her face. "Now I ran into Ernest and his friend Sam here while I was downtown. They're between homes now, but have some good looking dinner that they're willing to share. Don't you think it would be fine to share our space in return?"

"No, I don't think so!"

"Let's see what the Professor thinks, okay? Maybe he'll be able to help us decide." Rosine knew the best way to treat the excitable Gerald was to deflect his angst and bring in another opinion. "Hey Professor!" she yelled toward the second tent, "Can you come help us out here?"

Sam heard rustling in the tent and saw the leaves of the door push aside to reveal a smallish, pale man wearing thick frameless glasses stumble through the opening. He wore brown hiking boots with new laces on the left foot, cargo shorts, and a grey t-shirt that read, *Pluto RIP*. He held a hard-bound book in his hand – tattered and crumbling pages bound inside a faded red cover. Sam couldn't tell what the name of the book was, but he did see that it was thick and heavy and might be used as a weapon. He stood ready, just in case.

"I thought I heard a commotion out here, but I was hoping to study through it," he said in a high-pitched raspy voice. "What are you doing out here? Do you think you can keep it down a bit, you know I'm busy working on my dissertation!" What little hair the man had left appeared blown up from the back, presumably pasted to the back of his head by oil accumulated over several hot weeks without any real cleaning.

"Dammit, Edwin, this bimbo Rosine brought these two down here! They're gonna give us away and it's gonna be Rosine's fault! I think she should just send 'em back where she got 'em!"

"Professor Edwin, honey! Gerald is just sore at Ernest for a misunderstandin' about peeing in his port-a-john last winter. Besides, Ernest and Sam brought some dinner for us. I suspect, given their welcome so far, that they may want to head elsewhere to enjoy it, but I'm pretty hungry and I saw what they got – it looks pretty damned good. They just want to stay for a few days while they find their next place, and they promised that they wouldn't tell anyone about us or this place!"

Sam observed that this Edwin was certainly the leader of the trio, definitely the "alpha male" of the pack, even though he was physically smaller and weaker than Gerald. Rosine and Gerald were working to persuade the leader to their point of view, but the decision on whether Sam and Ernest could stay was clearly Edwin's. Sam found Edwin's authority to be a counter-intuitive social order within this group.

"Anyone stupid enough to pee in my port-a-john will be stupid enough to give us away! Let's send 'em off!" Gerald did not intend to be ignored.

"So," the *Professor* calmly asked Gerald, "this man, Ernest, peed in your port-a-john?"

Gerald nodded and ranted, "You're damn right he did. The bastard!"

"It was *your* port-a-john?" The Professor continued his questioning.

"It was my damned port-a-john, and he sure as hell did take a piss in it!"

"It was your *port-a-john*?" he asked once more, with greatly exaggerated emphasis.

"Yes!"

"And that seems so unreasonable to you? I would think that a port-a-john would be a proper place to urinate. I think we should let them stay for a night – especially because I am quite hungry and would like to have energy to continue my studies. Let's allow them to stay for tonight, yes?"

"Edwin! These two are *trouble!* You'll see. Besides, you always take Rosine's side. Damn! I just want to get my way, just once!" said Gerald, disappointed like a child overruled by his parent.

Sam saw that Rosine felt great satisfaction in her triumph over Gerald and she continued her diplomatic duties for the day.

"Why don't you gentlemen take a spot in my tent over here?" Rosine motioned toward the tattered blue dome. "I sleep on the left side, so you can have the right. Let's get your stuff set down in there, and then you can lay out the grub."

"Hurry your asses up," Gerald called as they ducked into the tent. "I'm damned hungry and not as gullible as Rosine, so that chow had better come through or we'll boot you back out faster than you can piss in my house! Bastard!"

Rosine's tent was not large. Sam had to duck to walk around, and Ernest had to resort to crawling on all fours. However, at floor-level, it was big enough for the three occupants to settle in and have enough room to stretch and lie down.

Rosine kept a few personal things at the far end where she rested her head when she slept. She had some photographs of people Sam assumed to be her relatives, a medicine bottle about half full of pills, a few blankets and a pair of high-heeled blue leather shoes. Sam found the shoes to be most interesting for a woman in Rosine's situation, and went over for a closer look.

"Hon, those are my old working shoes! I just kept 'em around in case I decide to come out of retirement. Probly won't ever wear 'em again, but you never know!"

"Ah'm more curious about that thar medicine bottle," Ernest jumped in. "There must be twelve different kinds of pills in thar. How do you keep 'em straight?"

"Oh, they're all pain pills," Rosine politely responded. "I get some pretty nasty headaches. Some days the red works the best, some days the yellow works the best. So, when my headache is coming on strong, I just take a couple of both. I add to my stock whenever I find something, so it's a nice mix."

"Ah'm hopin' them pills help yer headaches. I get 'em too, but mostly I jest need a snort o' the old Red Dawg to get past mine," Ernest grinned. "It's too damned bad ah'm all out. Ah'd jist need a sip 'er two."

Sam worried that Ernest might start dwelling on his lack of Red Dawg, but saw that his attention went back to Gerald as they could still hear him cursing outside the tent.

"Yer know, I don't think ole Gerry is gettin' over it," Ernest mused. "It's funny when I look back on it, but how wuz I ter know that wuz his house? He didn't have no sign or anything. Shit!"

"Don't you worry about Gerald," Rosine offered. "He'll get over it or he'll get used to it. Just put your stuff there. You know I don't mind sharing my room with a man or two if he has proper compensation. Let's get some of that food out to the kitchen and get us a meal!" Rosine folded her arms and smiled, adding, "It'll be nice havin' you boys here for a couple o' days."

Ernest picked up the bag of food as he and Sam followed Rosine, stepping around a faded plastic shopping cart and a makeshift clothesline to the tent next door. This one was larger than the other two and a tattered grey blanket was hung across the center with clothespins, informally dividing the space into a sitting area and Edwin's study/sleeping area.

"This here's our livin' room," Rosine explained, "we use this for a kitchen, and in the winter, we have a bit of heat here." Rosine nodded to a small electric space heater in the back corner.

"Hot damn," Ernest piped up sarcastically, "Yer have a heater in here, no doubt. I'll bet it did a helluva job this winter with no place to plug 'er in!"

"Things are not always what they appear, my friend," Edwin's voice came from the other side of the blanket wall.

"Edwin's right smart," Rosine stated. "He has it hooked up to the electric from the street light. He figured a way to tap into the wire there. Edwin sure figured it out, and then Gerald did the wiring one night last fall. He had to break open the base of the street light, but he did it! We've unplugged it for now 'cause there's no need for heat, and there's less chance someone will wander by and see it when it's not plugged in. But sometimes when we find something that needs cookin, we can plug back in and use that ol' iron for a hot pad. It can be a lot easier than startin' a fire for a small job. We just have to be quiet and careful when we pluggin' and unpluggin' so nobody notices. Edwin's pretty smart about all that, makin' us more comfortable and keepin' things quiet."

"*Stealthy*, we call it," Edwin's rasp broke in again. "I calculate that stealth is a key ingredient to the safety of our lifestyle here."

"Well, Mr. Stealthy, we're going to set up some supper in here," Rosine explained. "We'll call you from your studies when it's spread out."

Rosine found a tattered red and white checked tablecloth in the corner and spread it neatly on the floor of the tent, then broke out five mismatched plastic plates and dingy spoons. She placed the plates neatly on the tablecloth and put the spoons beside them, a la gourmet in a tent. Ernest took Rosine's cue and began parceling the bologna, cheese and bread onto the plates. He opened the bags of cheese puffs and popcorn, but didn't distribute them to the plates, thinking they might save until tomorrow if the crew didn't eat them all.

"Dinner's ready!" Rosine called.

"It damn well better be," Gerald grumbled as he shuffled toward Edwin's tent. "This better be caviar and crumpets if you're gonna be stayin' with us."

"Give it a rest, Gerry," Ernest spat as Gerald pulled back the flaps of the tent door. "Yer jist better sit and be thankful that I didn't piss on yer sandwich. I might've mistaken it for a port-a-john too!"

"I'll be glad to see you go. The sooner the better, you bastard," Gerald responded, still making not attempt at diplomacy. "This does look pretty good, though. It might be worth one night. Maybe."

"Well, maybe this'll help yer a bit," Ernest tossed the last three beers from the six pack to Rosine, Edwin and Gerald; he had already started on the fourth, "Sam, yer'll have to do without a beer tonight. I have a bit o' water here to share though. I hope that'll do yer well!"

Sam was not disappointed. He had acquired a taste for the foamy malt of beer after spending some time with Ernest, but he still preferred simple water. Also, the bubbles and foam bothered his nose. All things considered, Sam always preferred fresh, cool, water. He thought that Ernest knew that, and was simply working to make their hosts feel important. Being left out of the beer line was a diplomatic role that Sam didn't mind playing.

Sam made quick work of his bologna and cheese, choosing to eat them separately from his bread. He looked up after eating to see that Gerald and Edwin were also finished. They were all obviously famished. Starting in on the bag of cheese puffs, Edwin dumped nearly half the bag onto his plastic plate and handed the bag to Gerald. Gerald, his hard temper visibly softening without an empty stomach, poured a small pile on Sam's plate and started eating from the bag.

"Eat up, Sammy! Maybe you ain't so bad, even if you're hanging around with that bastard," Gerald, nodded toward Ernest, making sure he didn't get too comfortable. Yet, Sam could tell that Gerald's voice had come down from the tense pitch of just a few moments earlier. "Still, you'll need to head out in the mornin'. We have plenty goin' on, and don't need for you to take up our supplies or give us up to the outside."

Sam concluded that Gerald was softer but still not too friendly.

When the cheese puffs were gone, the group collectively leaned back from the tablecloth and passed the bag of popcorn around. Rosine motioned for Ernest to open his mouth, and threw a piece of popcorn toward him to catch. It bounced off Ernest's fuzzy cheek, causing him to roar with laughter as he picked it off the floor and stuffed it into his mouth. The two tried several times, with Ernest missing most but cackling wildly as the game continued.

"Juvenile," Edwin stated bluntly while rolling his eyes.

"Throw a few at ol' Sam thar," Ernest called to Rosine. "He'll even catch yer bad throws."

Rosine first threw a piece toward Gerald who missed in much the same style as Ernest, then toward Edwin who didn't even try to catch the piece in his mouth. Her shot bounced off his glasses then onto the ground where Edwin scooped it up. Rosine then changed targets to Sam, throwing at least ten pieces with varying levels of accuracy. Sam had no trouble catching them all.

"One of his many rare talents!" Ernest smiled at Sam. "He's his own person, no doubt!"

Sam was curious about why Edwin, Gerald and Rosine had decided to live in this communal fashion. His time on the street had shown him how unusual that arrangement was. Most *rough sleepers* were quite independent, whether by choice, drug habit or mental instability, and they preferred to stay to themselves. Sam had observed very few teams like he and Ernest, and this was the first group of three he had witnessed.

Evidently, Ernest was wondering the same thing. "How did yer all decide to live tergether like all this? Ya know Sam and me are a team. We can do diff'rent things and we help each other out. How der ya'll operate here?"

Rosine and Gerald hesitantly looked at Edwin for an okay, who looked around the circle and then finally nodded.

Rosine turned toward Ernest and Sam and her voice wavered as she began to explain.

"Late last year, I guess after Ernest pissed in Gerald's house ... Well, I was still working the street and still doing pretty good business. One night I found a date on Haskell Street and he drove into an alley by the impound yard for us to have some quiet time. It's secluded there, and he could just leave his car runnin' so we wouldn't get too cold. We went into the back seat for a bit more room. I was frozen enough from walkin' and was happy to be in with the heat no matter what I was doin'. So this guy, he has his time and then he went and got pretty irritated. That happens sometimes with guys, so I thought I was ready and just jumped for the door handle. That didn't do no good, though, 'cause I think he must have had his kid locks set on them back doors. So, that son-of-a-bitch just started poundin' on me inside his car. Then, by the grace o' God, Gerald happened by to see the ruckus. He pulled my door open an' dragged me out, then dragged that crazy man across the inside of the car and gave him a taste of the slappin' that he'd been lettin' loose on me."

"You know," Gerald piped in, "I had seen stuff like that all the time and it didn't really bother me. I'm not sure why I picked that time to stop."

"I guess I just have good taste in Guardian Angels!" Rosine smiled. Sam watched how Rosine looked at Gerald. He saw it formed from the same eyes, lips and teeth that she used for smiling at Ernest, but the smile for Gerald was deeper. It reminded Sam of the way his brothers and sisters would treat his mother when he was small.

"Gerald took care of that guy pretty good," Rosine continued, "but I was already broken up pretty serious. I could see blood coming off me from all over, and I could tell that my arm was broke. You know as well as I do that a trip to the doctor means a trip off the street, so I wasn't up for that. I told Gerald that I'd heal up just fine and I was much obliged for the help. But that crazy man just wouldn't let well enough alone."

"She needed help. She could hardly walk, and would have been picked up by the cops given how the blood was streaming everywhere. I couldn't just leave her to find her own way. Also, I had heard that there was a doctor living in the trunk of an old Mercury in the impound lot. Since we were right there, I figure we'd give it a go."

"Which is where *I* came into this picture," Edwin broke his silence. "Mind you I am *not* a Medical Doctor, but a Doctor of Philosophy. Well, really, I'm just a dissertation away from it. Try explaining that to a half-frozen, half-beaten working girl and the jolly green giant of the North Tulsa streets when they're banging on your trunk lid in the middle of the night."

"I still don't get it, Professor. Are you a doctor or not?" Rosine was still confused.

"Rosine, honey, a *medical* doctor is trained in the medical arts of healing. Other doctors are trained in other disciplines that may or may not be related to medicine. My doctorate will be in mechanical engineering, which I can assure you has minimal direct applicability for healing people. I might be able to design medical tools, but I do not make a habit of practicing medicine."

Rosine's quizzical look made it clear that she still didn't understand why someone who didn't know how to heal a person would be called "doctor".

"Don't worry about it, Rosine," Edwin sighed and continued the tale, "I had a nice set up in a '79 Mercury toward the middle of the impound lot. You see, most cars only stay in the impound lot for a short while – they're normally towed in from the street, having been crashed or illegally parked. Then, when the owner finds them, he pays the fine or storage fee and either drives the car away or has it towed to a repair shop. Last summer, I had taken to logging the cars coming in and out of the impound, because I was preparing a research paper on operational efficiencies. I would calculate the amount of time the car was in the impound lot, and was working to correlate it to other variables such as the make and model of the car, as well as the general condition of the vehicle when it was brought into the lot. Well, obviously the Merc jumped off the page when I found that it checked in, but never checked out. So, when fall hit with the cold snap I realized that it was just waiting around for me to move in. The trunk was huge – enough room for me and my books, and I could use a flashlight and read at night without being observed. A great home, certainly, albeit a little tight."

Gerald took back over, "Well, the word around the street was that there was a doctor living in the Merc, and I knew that this lady needed a doctor. So, I talked her into going to see him."

"Of course, I didn't know the first thing about treating this beaten woman," Edwin lamented, "but she was obviously in need, and I did have a first aid book in my collection. So, we just read through it based on her injuries. Gerald happened to have a nice bottle of vodka that we used for a disinfectant. We used electrical tape to hold several cuts together, and we used a sun visor from the inside of the Mercury as a splint for her arm, holding it on there with more tape. It wasn't a perfect situation, but we were able to get her patched up."

"Look at my arm!" Rosine boasted. "You can see that it's damn near straight. I am so grateful to these guys."

"After we treated her injuries, Rosine pulled thirty-five dollars from her brazier and handed it to me. She said it was my doctor's fee, and then she curled up in my trunk and went straight to sleep. Gerald and I watched over her that night. I was quite impressed with Gerald's sense of charity, having brought Rosine to me for treatment, however misguided. How often do you find a sincere *Good Samaritan*? As I thought it through, it seemed like we may be able to help each other out. I had already scouted this area and wanted to set up a camp here. I had a plan and had stashed the tents and equipment. However, I was concerned about finding food and with general security. I knew that if Gerald the Giant had a good enough heart to help out Rosine, he could handle the security. And, this beat up girl, sweet little Rosine, had just handed me $35. She had to have a way of bringing in cash when we needed it. So, we decided to stick together and make a go of it. I keep things running, Gerald makes sure nobody bothers us, and Rosine brings in the food. We take care of ourselves that way. We all have a purpose and a job. That's why we stick together out here."

"Well, you gents finish up your meal. We sure appreciate you bringing it to us here, and will put you up for a night's stay." Gerald went back into his role as the security officer of the crew. "But you know that you'll have to move along tomorrow. And, if you tell anyone about us, you'll have to deal with me. And, that won't be pretty."

Sam was disappointed. He looked into Ernest's eyes and could see that he was truly intimidated by Gerald. He had hoped that Ernest had arranged a new home for more than a night, however, one night was better than no nights, and Sam was grateful to have a roof for the evening.

6. Purpose

Sam listened to the sounds of the night in the clearing as he drifted in and out of a fitful sleep. He tried to doze on the pallet of blankets that he and Ernest had fashioned into a sleeping area on one side of Rosine's little blue tent. He was exhausted from the morning of panhandling and the afternoon of shopping and negotiation, yet his sleep was little more than quiet time to contemplate his situation.

He heard Rosine's slow breath, which was nearly drowned out by Ernest's raspy snoring. It wasn't unusually loud compared with other snoring Sam had witnessed, but it was a constant drone that could make sleeping a chore.

A light breeze blew through the tent. It was allowed to flow by a window-like opening on one end and the doorway on the other. Both openings were covered only by what was once a mesh to minimize the mosquito swarms. The mesh had been torn in some places and stretched in others, allowing a few fortunate blood suckers to feed on the tent's occupants overnight. Sam was relieved to see that most of the nasty bugs finding their way through the mesh were more attracted to Rosine than he or Ernest. Still, he did hear the occasional whine of wings circling his head.

Outside the light din of the tent, he could hear the buzz of the early cicadas in the surrounding trees. Sam found the cicadas to be a very interesting creature, being in possession of almost no means of defense, save their wings.

Of course their wings only worked when the creature was aware enough to use them, which seemed infrequent enough that both he and Ernest were often able to catch the bugs for entertainment. Sam had wondered whether the cicadas might be good to eat, but Ernest had chided him, indicating that they'd have to be "damned near starvin'" to resort to eating bugs. Sam hoped they wouldn't see that occur any time soon.

The song of the cicada ebbed and flowed for reasons that only the swarm would understand. It grew to a dull roar, then segued down to silence. During the periods of quiet, Sam listened to the water of the Arkansas River flowing south toward the Mississippi. The trickling sound was somewhat deceiving, as it would lead someone to believe there was a small creek flowing nearby. Yet in the early summer the river was nearly half a mile wide with a swiftly moving current.

Sam appreciated the chorus of the Oklahoma night, and drifted in and out of slumber. Sometimes waking to a loud stanza of cicada song, other times to a crescendo in Ernest's drone of snore. When he did wake, he would look for the outline of the half moon, shining brightly above the tent roof.

As the moon began to set in the west, Sam was awakened by another of Ernest's sleeping rants about missing his family. Sam had grown accustomed to these outbursts, as they were nearly a nightly occurrence, but he noticed that Rosine was startled and was staring wildly at Ernest as he sobbed and apologized in his sleep.

"Ah'm so sorry, Darlin'! I promise I'll stay erway from the hooch, an' I'll never smack yer never more. And, I'll find me a respectable job. Jest let me back, Honey. Them child's 'll be proud er me this time! Puhleeze, Darlin'!"

Tears came from Ernest's closed eyes as he slept and rehearsed the conversation for what had to be the thousandth time. Rosine's stare of fear shifted into a gaze of concern. Sam could tell that she empathized with Ernest's situation and truly felt for him. Nonetheless, everyone Rosine knew on the street had a sad personal tale. Everyone wanted just one more chance, but few would ever see it. She nodded at Sam. "You're a good egg for takin' care of ol' Ernest. He has a good heart, but a bad temper. I've had a man or two who hit me, but they didn't have the good sense to stay away when they couldn't control themselves. Maybe it's best for this family that Ernest keeps his distance."

Sam didn't have a strong opinion on that. He knew that Ernest got sad pretty frequently. Sometimes the Red Dawg would cheer him up, other times it would make him dangerous.

They could see flashes of lightening to the west now, and smell the storm blowing in. The noise of thunder began to mask the sound of Ernest's tirade, and he eventually settled into a deeper if still fitful sleep.

Rosine's eyes closed as Ernest's episode wound down, and Sam found himself sleeping peacefully, sheltered from the wind and rain, for the last couple of hours of night.

He woke to the fresh smell of dawn and the glint of the sun rising over the riverbank. He heard a light rustling in the reeds as he stretched his muscles off the pallet of blankets, and stepped outside to investigate.

The morning air was fresher and less humid outside the tent, and a light breeze came from across the river. He saw Edwin sitting on the remnants of an aluminum and mesh lawn chair, near the center of the triangle formed by the tents. Edwin was in a curious position: he sat with an unnaturally straight back and his legs folded across each other. His arms were raised evenly above his head with his hands cupped. His eyes were fixated across the clearing, staring intently at a small red fox poised to pounce. Despite his concentration on the fox, Edwin's peripheral vision found Sam, and Edwin smoothly looked toward Sam and put his finger across his lips to encourage continued silence, then returned to the fox. Sam moved quietly toward Edwin and then saw the object of the fox's breakfast plans. A grey cotton tail rabbit was peacefully munching on grass at the far edge of the clearing, oblivious to the fact that he was nearing his last breath. The fox, understanding that the rabbit would likely escape into the reeds and undergrowth, silently positioned himself so that when he pounced, the rabbit would either be caught immediately or be forced into the center of the clearing where there would be no place to hide. The fox, crouching, took a few more silent steps toward his quarry and stilled himself waiting for the precise moment to leap. Sam watched the fox's chest heave in and out, then tense after a final exhale. At this moment, with no additional hesitation, the fox leapt nearly ten feet horizontally while barely leaving the ground, landing with its jaws firmly around the rabbit's neck. In one final motion, the fox stood and shook it's head once, breaking the rabbit's neck. Sam saw the life evaporate from the rabbit's body before the rabbit ever knew of any danger. The fox, still either unaware of or unconcerned about Edwin and Sam's voyeurism, trotted silently away with breakfast dangling from his mouth.

Edwin untangled himself from his lotus position, and turned to Sam. "Now, that's nature at its finest. The strong and smart survive while the weak or stupid are eaten. What a wonderful setting, and a glorious way for both the fox and us to start our morning. I suppose the rabbit has seen better days though, wouldn't you agree? We are indeed fortunate to witness such a scene!"

Sam grinned back at Edwin. Indeed, it had been an interesting and strangely beautiful drama played out before them.

"I believe I will do a quick rinse and shave in the river to finish the wakeup routine." Edwin trotted away barefoot to the muddy riverbank. Sam had wondered why Edwin had appeared so clean-shaven. Having a water source, albeit the murky Arkansas River, had a number of advantages.

The zipper sealing Gerald's tent moved from bottom to top of the door, and the man-mountain stepped out, unable to stand upright until he had cleared the doorway. Yawning, he raised his arms in the air and stretched his hands into the sky. The stubble on Gerald's face was in significant contrast to the Professor's, but it seemed a natural part of Gerald's persona. It gave him a rough exterior, and likely made him look five years older than he would without the salt-n-pepper fuzz surrounding his face.

Gerald smiled into the sun, and yawned again. Sam was pleased to see that the gruff giant he met yesterday might have a more pleasant demeanor on this day. Sadly, though, when Gerald saw Sam in the courtyard, the smile became the same scowl he had worn throughout the evening.

"I guess you two are still here, huh." Gerald bypassed any friendly morning greeting. "I'm glad you have the sense to get up early to get your hide out of here. I hope your pal Ernest does the same before I have to rustle him out of Rosine's tent. If you don't want me to get rough with him, you'd better hurry him along."

Sam wasn't sure how to respond. He certainly didn't feel any pressure from Edwin to hurry out, and he was certain that Rosine wouldn't rush them back out to the street either. Sam took a quick drink of water, and stepped over to the riverbank with Edwin. Edwin had lathered up some soap and spread it across his face. He had scraped about half of the white foam from his face with a straight razor while squatting in ankle-deep water. Lumps of the foam were calmly circling in an eddy before being brushed into the swift-moving current farther out in the river.

"I suppose you've found that tact is not one of Gerald's strengths. We can't all be polished gentlemen. Unfortunately, while I do believe Gerald can be a bit hardheaded, I also believe he is correct on this occasion. We do appreciate your trade of food for the night. However, with more bodies here, we have a greater risk of being found. Further, we can hardly feed the three of us. Thinking about your two additional mouths makes us all uneasy. Rosine is the one that gathers most of our food, and I have seen what she can consistently provide. She's at her limit with we three. I'm sorry, my good fellow. I'm sure you'll find somewhere else suitable today. Just be careful if you go back into downtown – it's Monday and the streets will be busy. The drivers near this park are particularly aggressive and drive at high speeds. A collision around here could be fatal, so watch yourself and that crazy Ernest as well."

As if on cue, Sam heard Ernest's raspy voice in the clearing above them. His "good morning" had been an uncceremonious eviction notice, courtesy of Gerald. Sam was not surprised that Ernest didn't react well, and trotted back up to the courtyard to see how the discussion was progressing.

"Hot damn, Gerald!" Ernest was simply not a morning person. "Ah'm jest now wakin' up and yer already askin' mah to leave. I guess I'll jest not share mah breakfast with yer if yer t' be such a cantankerous host." Ernest grinned as he pulled a crumpled box of Pop Tarts from a side pocket of his knapsack.

Gerald just rolled his eyes. "You wouldn't have offered those anyway. You're just playin' us all. You want us to think you've got even more held back, and I know that's it. After those, you're down to empty!"

"Well, maybe I am, but I did plan ter share them 'tarts this mornin' too. 'Course, I did plan ter have a spell to wake up a little this morning too before Sam and I took our leave. Just ter show yer that I'm not just goin' on, here - have a 'tart. They're choc'lit!"

Ernest tossed one to Gerald and one to Sam, then when Edwin made his way from the riverbank, Ernest offered one to him as well.

"No, thank you, Ernest. Please split mine between Gerald and Rosine. I know they will both enjoy them."

Sam understood the loyalty that the simple gesture built for Edwin. It became clear that Gerald was Edwin's soldier and Rosine was Edwin's scout.

Rosine made her way from her tent, with a yawn and a smile. She found her Pop Tarts waiting in the courtyard, and obviously enjoyed the ready-made breakfast.

"Thanks, again Ernest. I can't believe you were holdin' that one out on me, but I'm glad you did. It was a nice surprise. We were happy to have you here as guests, *weren't* we Edwin and Gerald?"

"Of course we were," echoed Edwin.

Gerald simply grunted.

"Well, gents," she turned to Ernest and Sam, "I'm going to get myself put together so I can make my way uptown and do a little panhandling near the Civic Center. There's a software convention going on today and a concert tonight, so there should be some good opportunities. I'll walk with you back that way, if you'll wait a few minutes for me. Sound good?" She couldn't look at Ernest or Sam as she spoke.

Edwin also looked away, but Gerald stood erect, eyes on the outsiders with his arms folded across his chest.

"That'll be fine, Rosine. We're happy ter make yer all's aquaintance, an mebbie we can do some bis'ness again some time."

Ernest followed Rosine back into her tent. She went in to transform herself into a look for panhandling, and he to pack his blankets and other belongings into his knapsack.

Sam stayed in the courtyard and surveyed the pleasant area once more, following the line of reeds and underbrush surrounding the clearing. As his gaze approached the river's edge, he noticed another rabbit quietly eating grass and weeds. Sam knew he was quicker than most any of the other *rough sleepers* he interacted with, but he really had no concept of whether he could approach a wild animal as the fox did and have any chance of catching it. He didn't really consider the rabbit to be food - Sam's stomach was full, and the rabbit wasn't wrapped in paper or foil like any other modern food. However, attempting to catch the creature just seemed *fun* at the moment.

Sam heard Edwin whisper, "Watch this!" to Gerald as Sam silently left the courtyard, circled the tent and worked to position himself so that the rabbit would have few places to go if his first pounce missed. The wind was still blowing slightly over the river, and Sam realized that the rabbit would likely not smell him approaching. He studied the creature's build - the rabbit's eyes were on the sides of its head, likely giving it better vision to the rear. Sam stepped closer and closer, stopping silently if the rabbit looked up or sniffed the air. Somehow Sam knew to halt his approach and remain still when the rabbit looked up to check his surroundings. Approaching from the rear, Sam thought that the river would prevent the rabbit from running directly away, and a large tree would keep it from darting to the left, so he aimed his jump slightly to the right of the animal and leapt.

Sam's jump was slow and klutzy compared to the fox, yet it caught the rabbit by surprise. As he expected, the rabbit attempted to dart to the right, and after the initial pounce, Sam was able to grab the rabbit's hind leg and throw it toward the river into more of a corner between the water and the tree. He then pounced again, actually catching the rabbit near the neck as he had seen the fox do. Sam was so surprised to have a good handle on the squirming animal that he was unaware of the pain and blood pouring from where the rabbit's teeth were sunk into his own flesh. Once that realization hit, he instinctively shook the rabbit and felt a quick crack as the animal fell limp. The adrenaline pumping through him kept him smiling, even as he noticed

Edwin and Gerald laughing uncontrollably and slapping each other on the back. Neither could believe that Sam had actually caught the rabbit, but they were more entertained by the two-pounce process and the fact that Sam was so surprised when the creature fought back.

Ernest and Rosine hustled out of the tent to see what the guffaws were about, and were amazed to see a smiling Sam trotting back up toward the tents holding a dead rabbit.

"Well, hot damn! I knowed Sam were a quick ol' boy, but never dreamed he'd catch damned a rabbit!" Ernest grinned at Sam. "Bring that ol' varmit up here, and we'll make us some lunch outta him! I loves me some roasted rabbit!"

The three tent dwellers were in shock, but Ernest saw the opportunity. If Sam could catch a rabbit every once in a while, Ernest could clean and cook it, and they would have a supporting role in the clearing. Like Rosine, they could be providers.

"I'm not eatin' any dead varmit like that!" Gerald saw Ernest's motives and groused, "Besides, Sam'll never catch another one. He just got lucky with a stupid rabbit. The next one won't be so dumb!"

Edwin was more in Sam and Ernest's corner. "Let's give this a try, Gerald. You know there are plenty of rabbits around here except in the dead of winter. They could prove to be a good food supplement if these two can really make it happen. I'm a bit more concerned about whether Ernest can make a meal out of this first one than whether Sam can catch another one later. Sam has already shown us what he can do."

"Come on, Sam! I'll show yer how I do it." Ernest had no confidence problem here. "We'll show ol' Gerry and Edwin that we kin do 'er up right. Rosine! Kin I borrow that knife o' yurs?"

"Sure Ernest. Just bring it back clean like you got it."

"Ah'l bring 'er back clean, along with a nice clean varmit to boot!"

Sam was excited that they may have an opportunity for more time in the camp. Ernest led Sam to an area on the riverbank just downstream of their encampment and the bridge, taking advantage of the bridge itself for camouflage. He knelt near the water and fumbled through the skinning and cleaning process. Sam looked on, but did not participate. He was interested, but not interested enough to jump in and help. He studied the skinned carcass laid neatly on the soft grass of the riverbank as Ernest cleaned the knife in the murky waters of the Arkansas River.

Ernest carried the cleaned animal by the hind legs back to the camp, smiling broadly at Gerald and laying the creature in the frying pan over the morning fire.

The meat started to smell good as it cooked, and Rosine appeared with a glass salt shaker, the silver top dented in numerous places from years of abuse in whatever restaurant it had served before Rosine acquired it. She tapped the shaker in her palm to break the chunks of salt back into granules that would make their way through the holes in the lid. She shook what she deemed to be an appropriate amount onto the meal, and Ernest gave her a nod. A few minutes later, Ernest took the pan from the fire and cut the rabbit into five chunks, of mostly equal size.

'Here yer go, Lady and Gents," Ernest almost sang as he offered pieces of the catch to each of his audience. "Bone appétit, I always say!"

The rabbit actually did taste good, and Sam wolfed his down quickly, nearly consuming the bones along with the meat. The size wasn't all that impressive, and Sam judged they would need about 3 rabbits to actually make a meal for this group. He saw the others enjoying the meat as well.

Edwin smiled as he ate. "Well, gents, I guess you can have a place. I won't promise it to be permanent, but if you can contribute, we're fine with you being here."

"It isn't permanent, for sure," Gerald scoffed, obviously not as excited. "Rosine, I hope you're okay sharing your tent with these two, 'cause they aren't coming into mine!"

"I'd love to," Rosine answered, licking her fingers as she finished her portion of the rabbit.

"We do need to talk through some of our operating rules," Edwin said, straight to business. "Given your chosen lifestyle on the street, I'm a bit concerned that you won't be able to abide by these, but they are our rules nonetheless."

Sam watched Gerald drop his cleaned rabbit bones into the fire, rise, and stand beside Edwin with his arms folded, ever the enforcer.

"They're pretty simple," Edwin went on, "One, you must not speak of our location to outsiders. Two, you must take great care when entering and exiting our space not to call attention to your trip. Three, you must continue to contribute. Four, you must stay far from the police or others who would evict us from this area. Anything important that I've missed, Gerald?"

Gerald shook his head, staring deeply and menacingly at Sam and Ernest. "Okay, then, after that nice meal, I will retire to my tent to study. Have a nice day!" And he was gone.

Sam smiled from head to foot, and both Ernest and Rosine could tell that he was relieved to have another home.

P.D. Bruns

7. Summer Heat

The warm days of May grew longer and more humid, and they eventually became the scorching hot days of June and then July. The temperatures were oppressive, even in the shade of the bridge, so the group was far less active while the sun was out. The hot weather also brought new animals to the clearing. Both Edwin and Rosine had found snakes in their tents. Sam had killed the one in Rosine's tent, breaking its neck in a way resembling his rabbit kills. He thought it might be useful for a meal, but the rest of the group had decided that it was not good for eating. Edwin had chased one from his tent using a physics textbook.

The water in the river had also receded significantly, as the snowmelt from the Rocky Mountains, many miles upriver, was exhausted. The spot where Sam had once enjoyed getting a drink directly from the river was now dry dirt, not even mud, and it crunched beneath his feet. He now had to walk another fifty or so feet to get refreshment. Sam did not mind the walk so much, but when Gerald or Ernest or Rosine had to fetch water for the camp, they complained incessantly. Of course, getting a bucket full of water for the camp was a bit more work than just getting a drink. Further, it carried some element of risk, as a person carrying a bucket of water from the river might be seen as suspect by someone passing by. Any of the group carrying water from the shrinking river took extra care to go late in the evening or early in the morning to avoid detection.

During these months, Sam and Ernest would set out early, watching for rabbits that put themselves in a vulnerable position. Once Sam or Ernest would spot one, they would both walk around the animal to corner it near the water, then Sam would pounce. Sam had become smoother with practice, and was also much more deliberate about breaking the animal's neck after catching it. He found that the sooner the animal died, the less likely it was to fight back. Ernest had even tried the technique, but he wasn't quick enough to get close to one of the animals.

As the heat of the summer continued, Sam and Ernest discovered fewer rabbits to be had. As a result, squirrels became a secondary target. Of course, the squirrels were less desirable than the rabbits because they could climb trees, they provided less meat, and they tended to fight more viciously when caught. While Ernest seemed to be able to keep the rabbits and squirrels separate, Sam just saw the squirrels as smaller, noisier and more agile rabbits.

One morning, Sam felt very pleased to have cornered a very large "rabbit" between the river and a wall of the Twenty Third Street Bridge. Sam knew that he had the animal in a place where it could not escape and stealthily called out to get Ernest in to complete their trap. Ernest took his place and his eyes widened when he saw the quarry, a larger black mammal with a white stripe down its back. Sam thought it curious that the rabbit appeared unconcerned with Sam and Ernest taking position on him in this way. Ordinarily, a rabbit or even a squirrel in this position understood that its life might be near an end, and began looking for a means of escape, but this one simply waved it's big, bushy tail and continued digging at a hole it found to be interesting.

Sam, still very pleased, grinned back at the wild-eyed Ernest and began to slowly step forward, moving in for the kill. The animal looked up and took note of Sam, but still was unconcerned and went on about its business of digging around the hole. As he did, Sam noticed that Ernest did not follow his lead in stepping toward the meal. Further, Ernest's face had become red and he began motioning at Sam to come back. Ernest stayed quiet, but was curiously animated and jumping around in a frenzied way. Sam had known Ernest to act irrationally when on a binge of the Red Dawg, but today this was not the case. Regardless, Sam pressed ahead into position, cornered his quarry against the bank of the river and began his well-practiced pounce. As he felt the fur of the animal in his grasp, Sam suddenly found himself to be completely blind, seeing only an angry bright light all around. As his brain processed the sudden lack of vision, a secondary sensation of unimaginable burning in his eyes began to register. Sam was unable to focus on his prey, and immediately fell to the ground covering his eyes and wailing in agony. He continued to see the light, a painfully bright light, whether his eyes were open or closed. He rubbed his eyes, but that was no help. He found his face to be damp, as though the animal had urinated on him. And the smell was beyond any foul urinary odor he had ever experienced. The stench was now permeating his lungs, monopolizing his sense of taste. Between his own wails of pain, Sam could hear hollering from Ernest and Rosine back up near the tents. He could not understand what they were trying to tell him, as his senses were completely overloaded. He also could not understand why they did not come to his assistance. Surely the needles he felt in his eyes could be removed. Surely he wouldn't be blinded for life. Yet, without assistance from the others, and unable to shake the pain by rubbing his eyes, Sam simply rolled about on the moist sand of the riverbank. Back and forth he went, unable to control himself, only wishing for some relief from the pain, stench and putrid taste in his mouth.

Sam's writhing on the riverbank eventually rolled him over the edge and into the water. Under any other circumstances, Sam would make every effort to drag himself from the water as quickly as he could. However, on this day, the cool of the water began to dull the pain in his eyes and gave some relief from the smell of the liquid. He took a breath, as best he could, and submerged himself completely, wondering if a drowning death might be preferable to the agony he was feeling on the bank of the river. He stayed under the water as long as he could, and then slowly raised his head for a quick breath.

As his eyes broke the water, he found the bright light was fading to blurry images of the world around him, and the black rabbit had vanished. He also found that he had an audience. Ernest, Rosine and Gerald were all pointing at him and laughing uncontrollably. Sam found nothing about the situation to be laughable, and was more than a little perturbed to have his anguish be the center of entertainment for these three.

Ernest was laughing so hard, he could barely catch his breath to speak. "Hot damn, Son!" he panted, "I was tryin' ter warn yer! Don't yer know what a damn skunk is? I'll bet yer have a purdy good idear now, don't cher?"

And with that Ernest, Rosine and Gerald hooted and laughed and held their bellies as Sam wallowed in the shallow, muddy water of the Arkansas River. Sam would certainly not forget what a skunk was and what it could do. This pain was not worth a meal, not even a fine one. And, if the animal tasted that bad on the outside, it probably tasted even worse to eat. The black animal with the white stripe would be permanently removed from Sam's list.

Sam did find it interesting that this was the first time he had seen Gerald laugh. Actually, it was the first time he had ever seen him smile a happy smile. Too bad it came at such a painful cost for Sam.

Even with his immediate bath in the river, Sam carried the smell of the encounter for nearly a week. There was no hunting, as any potential prey could smell him coming long before Sam could see them. He was ostracized by his friends, because his smell made them nauseous. Sam found that ironic, as the other four were certainly capable of emitting a colorful olfactory bombardment on any given day.

Rabbit hunting didn't improve significantly, even after the smell from the skunk faded, and so Rosine began inviting Sam to go on panhandling trips with her. Like the Arkansas River, her earnings from panhandling were shrinking in the heat. Rosine still brought some groceries home almost every day, but she complained that folks were unwilling to roll their car windows down and give to her when the heat would creep into their car. Edwin, working to manage Rosine, told her to use the heat to look more pathetic. Sam didn't think that would help, since Rosine was already truly blessed with talent when it came to looking pathetic.

Sam resisted Rosine's constant invitations, instead opting for walks by the river or feigning feeling ill. However as his rabbit hunting productivity faded, he felt pressure from the group to contribute.

Not surprisingly, Gerald soon stated his mind. "If Sam and Ernest don't come up with some food, we may need to do a reduction in force!" he blurted one evening as the five settled down on the ground between the tents. "What d'ya think, Edwin? Time for the visitors to go? Seems they've overstayed their welcome and usefulness, don't cha think?"

Edwin didn't voice agreement, but didn't argue in Sam and Ernest's favor either. He simply rubbed his chin and looked from Gerald to Sam to Ernest and back to Gerald. He shook his head at both, and retired to his tent for the evening.

Seeing what was coming, Ernest responded to the pressure by cobbling together a half bottle of Red Dawg over the next several days. He didn't have money to buy one, but he started with a trickle in a bottle, and went exploring around the riverside trash cans to add to his supply. He would find half a swallow in one bottle, maybe just a nip in another, and continued to pour the traces of liquid into his bottle. He didn't worry that some of the traces may have been more backwash than Red Dawg. He didn't worry that some of the bottles were simply vodka or whiskey either. If he could smell a trace of alcohol in the source, he dumped it into his consolidated bottle. He knew he could convince himself that the bottle was pure enough when he settled down to drink it. He had to focus to keep from nipping at the bottle as he filled it, but he knew the effect would be greater if he could hold off until he had half a bottle together for a single sitting. After a few days of foraging, Ernest had brought no food home to the group, but he had amassed enough liquor in the Red Dawg bottle to have a meaningful binge.

The evening Ernest completed his Red Dawg bottle assembly went the way so many before it had gone. He and Sam came into the campsite as the sun was setting over the west bank of the Arkansas River. The shadow of Lookout Mountain drew the shape of an "A" in the red-orange horizon. The trickle of the river was barely audible, and the humidity was oppressive. The cicadas' sound in the tall trees was somewhat muted compared with their song earlier in the summer. Nonetheless, it dominated the other sounds of the evening. Gerald was the first to see the pair, and observing Ernest's no bounty for the evening, was the first to put a shot across the bow.

"I see you boys are coming home empty handed again. I don't think we can keep carrying you. You know you have to produce to stay. Edwin, I think it's time to send this worthless pair on their way."

Edwin, playing the sage, again simply rubbed his chin.

With Edwin in a silent mood, Gerald added, "What have you boys been doing all day, if you're not bringing some food home? You just been wandering around aimlessly? You'd think you were homeless or something! I'm here to tell you that it's about time for you to go."

"Gerald, yer a sumbudabitch." Ernest had heard enough. "Yer ain't mah mama, and yer ain't mah boss. Sam and ah, here, have brought yer many a meal. Us fellers is jist havin' a rough spell. Yer'd think yer would be a bit more understandin'. Yer been livin' off us and Rosine for quite a while too. I don't see yer out chasin' food with us or 'handlin' with Rosine, so quit yer bitchin'!"

"Enough!" The exchange was enough to goad Edwin into the conversation. "Gerald, these gentlemen did bring us a good number of meals. We should be thankful for their contributions and treat them with respect..."

"Damn right! Yer tell 'im..." Ernest piped in, only to be cut off.

"Yet," Edwin continued forcefully, "you have produced very little in recent times. We have to expect you continue to help us, or you cannot stay. While Gerald has no tact and is overly direct, he is also correct. If you cannot be productive in the next five days, we will ask you to find another place of residence. I think five days is fair at this point."

Tact or no tact, Gerald knew enough to simply gloat silently, as additional words from him could get no better result. His arms were crossed and his head held high. He knew that with the rabbit population hunted out, he had numbered Sam and Ernest's days in the camp.

Rosine bowed her head, looking toward a random spot on the ground. She knew that Edwin was wise and knew when to push, but her caretaker instincts gave her pause. She felt responsible for bringing the two into the camp, but also knew that they had really amounted to two extra mouths to feed through the last couple of weeks. The evening ended quietly, as the important words had been spoken. Sam retired to Rosine's tent as the sun set, while Ernest stayed outside to start his date with the Red Dawg bottle. While Sam tried to sleep, he knew Ernest's intentions and restlessly listened as Ernest put his plan into motion.

It started with a few long draws on the bottle. Sam winced, knowing the impurity of Ernest's concoction. He understood Ernest's pain was so acute that he didn't care what was mixed in with the Red Dawg. He could hear Ernest breathe a deep, "Ah!" after each long pull. He could hear Ernest burp loudly a few times after the alcohol began to numb his thoughts and actions. He could hear Ernest stumble around the camp, and begin a mix of a rant and a sob as the buzz turned into a full-blown bender. Sam knew it was only a matter of time before Ernest's mind would turn to his family.

And so it was, as the twilight shifted to darkness. "Aw, Shondra Lee, I'm sorry! Puhleeze, take mah back. I'll do better this time. Honest, I will. I'll work hard, an I'll take care o' them kids too. I'll be a good husband ter ya! I'll be a good daddy to them kids! I'll promise to yer that I've changed…"

Ernest rattled on and Sam worried that he would become too noisy and cause Gerald or Edwin to cast them off yet tonight. His worry was justified. Ernest grew louder with each new sip. He transitioned between begging for Shondra Lee's forgiveness and cursing the moon and the summer night sky for all his problems. Ernest's rant become louder and more foul as the night drew on.

As Ernest continued his binge, Sam knew this would be the fiercest wrath of Red Dawg he had yet to witness. He heard the last swallow and prolonged, "Ah!" followed by the smash of the bottle against a concrete bridge pillar as Ernest discarded the bottle. He then heard Ernest continue the rant. The intoxicated man wailed at the half moon, screamed at the light summer breeze and cursed the song of the cicadas. Not unexpectedly, his soliloquy eventually returned to the familiar lament for Shondra Lee. "Take mah back, honey! I'll take good care o' yer from here out. No more o' the Red Dawg, jist work and care fer yer. That's it! Puhleeze, honey!'

Sam knew Ernest's noise was too much, echoing across the river. At that level, it was likely to attract unwanted attention from the surrounding area. As that thought sank in, a voice came from high upon the bridge. It was a late-night pedestrian putting in his own opinion on Ernest's rant. "Shut up, you old drunk! No wonder that honey of yours doesn't want you around! You're noisy as hell! Just shut up, or go talk to someone who cares!"

"Yer shut yer mouth, yer little bastard! Come down here and say that to mah face, if yer mean it!" Ernest shot back, "I'll tear yer apart like – "

With a muted thud, Ernest was silenced. Sam poked his head out of the tent, wondering what the stranger on the bridge had done to Ernest to quiet him so suddenly. He was surprised to see Gerald carrying Ernest across the scrub brush into the common area between the tents. Gerald softly laid him down on the grass as Edwin came in behind, holding a worn, wooden baseball bat in his hands. Sam tried to hide his rage, and thought about charging them both, but knew he would get the same treatment if he attempted.

"Settle down, my young Sam," Edwin counseled, "I would not have struck him if it could have been avoided. You know that we cannot have our location given away to the public, and we certainly cannot become a nuisance to the area. This was the simplest way to silence him. He'll have a headache in the morning when he wakes, but he'll not be able to tell if it came from this bat or from that bottle. Either way, he inflicted upon himself. Remember, five days or it's time to leave."

Sam felt like he understood the significance of the situation. He was also seriously concerned about Ernest's ability to be of any help tomorrow. Between the Red Dawg and the smack on the head, Ernest was not likely to be moving around with any purpose in the morning.

As Edwin and Gerald retired to their tents, Sam watched Rosine tenderly tuck a rolled up blanket under Ernest's head to serve as a pillow. She then covered his arms and face with another light blanket to help deter the mosquitoes that were hovering around the unconscious man, looking for the best place to take a draw of alcohol-laden blood.

Sam slept lightly the rest of the night, worrying that the stranger on the bridge would follow the sound down to the camp, or that Gerald or Edwin might take up the baseball bat against Sam or Ernest in their sleep, just to finish them off. The violence they displayed had certainly eroded the trust Sam had for them, and he no longer felt safe sleeping in this camp. Sam decided that it would be best to move on, five days in the camp or not, and resolved to encourage Ernest to move out with him in the morning, effectively wagering that the evil they knew about in the camp was greater than the evil they did not know about elsewhere in the city. Sam was afraid to leave this place, but even more afraid to stay.

P.D. Bruns

8. Happenstance

The sun rose a bit farther to the south on this morning, since the summer was fading into autumn. At the mouth of the concrete culvert that Sam and Ernest now inhabited, Sam could feel what could even be called a cool breeze.

"It's still a great spot. A great spot, ain't it Sam?" Ernest grinned over at Sam from his sleeping pallet. "It'll suit us fine 'til the corps boys decide ter let a lotta water outter the dam up yonder. We just have ter be ready to move out if we hear them corps sirens. Ah'm jist glad yer can hear as good as yer can. Yer keep listenin', ya hear?"

Upon being evicted from the campsite near the Twenty Third Street Bridge, Ernest had suggested that they take up temporary residence in an old outlet pipe on the west side of the river. By now, Sam had come to realize that *everything* was temporary.

The outlet pipe from the now closed EastOK refinery was a full six feet across and had once carried production waste water from the refinery into the river. The government, of course, had outlawed such dumping long ago. The refinery had been closed for many years, and the steel grate guarding the outlet was rusted to the point where one could wiggle it open across its remaining mounting bolts and squeeze into the pipe. The grate kept the casual observer from wandering in, and the dark of the pipe kept the occupants from being easily visible.

When they first moved in, Sam and Ernest had to evict several water moccasins. The snakes were not pleased to be forced on their way, nor were the colonies of spiders and other crawling critters. Having now been here more than a month, however, they had a full ten feet of pipe cleaned and somewhat livable from the front grate to the second pipe joint. The pipe's aging concrete had partially collapsed above that joint, so the area above it was much less hospitable anyway. Ernest hadn't made his way up there, and Sam had absolutely no interest in exploring the dank area above the collapse. The pipe had actually been cooler than the campsite through the last part of the summer, as it was thick concrete, mostly covered by earth. It also had a wonderful view across the river that made for very enjoyable sunrises. With the refinery closed yet still surrounded by a chain link fence, the only human visitors were stray kids who occasionally found their way through holes in the old fence, looking for mischief. They were typically there for a thrill, and were easily scared away by a noisy Sam and Ernest when they introduced themselves as the "armed guards of the facility."

All in all, it was a great place. However, Sam and Ernest considered it temporary in that it would only be a great place until the water started running swiftly in the Arkansas River from the autumn rains. When that happened, the river would rise above the mouth of the pipe, putting it under water again. That danger was always present, and Sam and Ernest made a habit of staying ready to travel, keeping an eye on the river, and keeping their ears open to hear the sounds of the Army Corps of Engineers sirens. The sirens signaled that the Corps was letting water out of the Keystone Dam about twenty miles upriver, and that the water would soon be rising.

Sam had heard the sirens twice since the pair took up residence in the pipe. Both times, he had alerted Ernest and they climbed out onto the top of the pipe with all their belongings to keep watch on the river. Both times, they watched the river rise, but fortunately not enough to flood the pipe.

"I know yer listenin' fer that flood siren. Yer a good feller and I appreciates yer," Ernest rambled on. "Let's go see if we can scare us up a rabbit fer a meal terday. I know they've been hard ter find, but I think it's worth a go, don't yer?"

Sam was hungry, and agreed that it was worth an attempt.

The pair strolled along the west bank of the river, staying between the well-traveled bike path and the bank of the river itself. The grass near the path was well-manicured, as public parks go. The neatly trimmed grass gave way to wilder grass, which became even wilder as it approached and grew between the grey limestone rocks lining the river's edge. This grass had grown tall through the summer, nearly to a man's knees in many places. Yet, with the intense heat and customary lack of rain in the late summer, the grass was baked to a yellow-brown hue, with edges sharp enough to slice tiny paper cuts on exposed skin that passed by the blades in just the right direction. If a rabbit was to be found, it would be hiding in the thick, brown grass, waiting for a quiet opportunity to sneak nearer to the path to snack on the juicy green grass and weeds kept moist by human irrigation.

The two worked the west bank all the way from their drainage pipe to the walking bridge, more than a mile downriver. They beat the grass and noisily trudged across the rocks, hoping to drive a meal into the open. In doing so, they scared up innumerable insects, several mice and at least a half-dozen snakes. However, there was not a rabbit to be found on this day. Nothing. Both Sam and Ernest could feel their stomachs churning, having been empty for some time. Sam was feeling desperate. Ernest noticed.

"Awl right, Sam. We ain't gonna find no rabbits here, so let's find us a corner and see what we can rustle up thar."

Sam was relieved that Ernest was willing to spend some time panhandling. It really wasn't as much fun as chasing the rabbits, but it almost always provided enough for a small bite to eat, and that's what was really on Sam's mind.

"R'member that corner near the square that Rosine used to stay near? That's not far off, and thar'll be enough traffic to make it worth our while." Ernest went on, "We'll get enough to score a sammich and a swig of Red Dawg and we'll be cooler than punch! Let's head that way, you old scoundrel!"

And so they set off across the walking bridge. The bridge, open only to pedestrian and bicycle riders, was really a decommissioned railroad bridge put to good use as a fishing pier, a jogging path and a lovers rendezvous. It spanned the nearly half-mile width of the river bed, though water only ran under the bridge as a trickle in a few lower-lying areas during this time of year. The width of the bridge was only the width of a railroad track, so while Sam and Ernest crossed toward the east, persons crossing to the west could not put a natural distance between themselves and the grungy pair of *rough sleepers*. While it was probably uncomfortable for the joggers and lovers and families to pass within a few inches of Sam and Ernest, it was curious to Sam to have the strangers that close to him. He could smell the soaps and perfumes on the clean people, and he found the odors quite interesting. Children, some in strollers and wagons pulled by their parents, often smiled and waved at Sam. However, the parents invariably maintained a blank stare a few feet ahead of Sam and Ernest as they walked, and tightened any grip they had on the children's hands. The parents were careful to minimize their children's exposure to the filth of the homeless and the danger that such deviant personalities might bring.

Once across the bridge, the pair continued on the asphalt jogging trail toward downtown. Bicyclists, joggers and families still passed by. With the additional space of the trail, however, it was evident that they gave a wide berth. Sam made a mental note that he enjoyed the bridge, largely for the forced closeness of the people around him. It wasn't that he was feeling predatory or wanted to cause injury to the people around him, he just wanted to experience that closeness, albeit forced, to others.

The trail curved as it stayed parallel to the river, and it widened in certain areas to let bicycle traffic more easily pass by the walkers and joggers. As they passed a particularly wide part of the trail, Sam noticed Ernest come to an abrupt stop and begin coughing as a woman and her two children approached. The larger child was half his mother's size, and was riding a small, dusty bicycle that was actually a bit too small. The boy was unconcerned with the improper fit, and continually sped forward, then turned around to go back to his mother. He loved the rush of the speed, but also stayed obediently close to his mother on the trail.

The mother pushed the smaller child in a tattered stroller, while the little girl's feet dangled below the footrests but above the pavement. Her socks didn't match, and she only had one shoe on. Sam could see the other shoe tied to the push bar of the stroller with the Velcro that was intended to hold it on the child's foot. The mother doted on the little girl, and sauntered down the trail, enjoying the morning sun despite the heat already building in the air.

Ernest continued his coughing fit, and covered himself as the three went by. While there was ample space available, the woman passed relatively close to Ernest. She looked longingly at him, and stroked the small child's hair with her free hand as they passed. Then she stopped and pressed a few green bills of cash into Ernest's grubby hand. She whispered something at Ernest, but Sam couldn't understand what she said. She then nodded and passed along, again attending to her children and keeping the boy close by on his bicycle.

A full five minutes passed before Ernest began to move again. Sam could see drops of water leaking from the corners of his eyes, and could hear him muttering to himself as he stood still. Bicyclists and joggers swerved around him since he appeared to be planted in the center of the trail. When Ernest finally did begin to move again, it was a slow shuffle with the small wad of cash clinched firmly in his left palm.

Ernest found his way to the first available park bench, taking a place at the opposite end from a young couple lacing their jogging shoes. The couple departed promptly, allowing Ernest to stretch out on the bench, pressing his face into the corner between the backrest and the seat. He began to shake as he sobbed on the bench. Sam didn't understand, and so he sat on the ground near where Ernest had his face pressed through the seat of the bench and patiently waited.

Ernest eventually collected himself, but his words were muffled as he refused to pull his face away from the bench. "Sam, yer gotta know, that wuz mah Shondra Lee. She's so good to let mah near them kids. She knows I don't mean 'em no harm, but she also knows they don't need to see mah lookin' like I do." Ernest was genuinely sad now. This was not like the rants he would have about Shondra Lee when the Red Dawg was talking. Here, the sobs were quiet and the pain clear, without the blur of the alcohol. "She's a good mama! She's doin' what she can for them kids. She knows that I ain't worth a damn, but she's still human to mah. I don't deserve all that. I know that I ran out on her and I don't take care of her or them kids. I know that I'll make it up to her one day. Jist one day. Jist one day!"

Sam sat beside the park bench, and continued his wait while Ernest wept and silently came to terms with his situation. While the sun rose in the sky and the day became hotter, Ernest didn't move. Finally, his eyes dried and he realized the day was half over. Ernest could cry no more, and so he sat back up on the bench.

"Well, Sam. Ah'm sorry yer had to watch all that. I miss mah Shondra Lee and mah kids, but I knows I ain't no good fer 'em. Let's go on up ter that 'handlin' spot and see if we can get us enough fer a meal and some Red Dawg."

Another thirty minutes of walking up the trail, and then on the side-streets into downtown brought them to a nice corner with a wide sidewalk and a timed stop light. Ernest had learned from Rosine that the best corners for panhandling were those with a lot of automobiles, a place to sit, and an older stoplight that didn't have any traffic sensors on it. The timed stoplights, were better suited to panhandling because they would stop cars without regard to the flow of traffic. The smarter, sensor-based lights would stay green for the busier road until traffic appeared from the smaller road, and so there were inevitably fewer stopped cars as prospective customers.

Ernest had picked up a cardboard box from the Dumpster at the Grocery Stop on the way, which he now tore into a single flat piece of cardboard and used the stub of a black crayon to scribble his message to the corner, "Will work for food".

Sam didn't understand what Ernest was working to accomplish with the sign. The pair had absolutely no intention of working, so it seemed pointless to him.

"Don't yer worry, Sam. Ah've used signs like this before. There ain't nobody that wants to put yer ter work. They jist want yer to not bother them. Signs like this do a lot better than ones that say, 'I don't have no job, and I cain't seem ter keep straight, can I have some of yer money?" Ernest explained, "And it's a lot shorter message too!"

Ernest took up position on the corner. He sat on the warm concrete and leaned back against the pole of a street sign indicating: "Right Lane Must Turn Right." He was facing the traffic, working to look at any driver or passenger that was stopped within a car or two of him.

"Be sure to look hot and tired and pathetic, thar Sam," Ernest coached, "That'll help git us our due! Ah'm damned good at lookin' pathetic – it comes natural to mah! Also, be sure to look 'em in the eye. Thatta way they know yer really see 'em."

The pair spent the remainder of the day working the corner. When the traffic would stop, Sam and Ernest would look as tired and pathetic as possible and work to make eye contact with the occupants of the cars. If a driver made eye contact,

Ernest would saunter over to the window and make a "rolling down" motion with his hand. If the driver put down their window, Ernest would politely ask, "Do yer have any work for an ol' boy like mah to do? Ah'm right handy, yer know, especially when I ain't hungry," he would start. Then, he would follow with, "Well, if yer don't have any work fer me, would yer mind helpin' me make a down payment on a cheeseburger? It would go a long way." And he would typically collect a sprinkle of pocket change.

Ernest knew that the customers wouldn't want to touch his gloved hand, so he always offered his hat as a place to put the donation. He always kept two singles in the hat to give the impression that others had donated paper money, and make sure that customers would feel obligated to donate a little more change as opposed to just a few pennies. At the end of the afternoon, the collection tally was thirty-two dollars and forty-three cents, including the eight dollars that Shondra Lee had pressed into Ernest's hand earlier in the day.

"Sam, I think we have enough fer now. Let's go get some grub and some drink, don't yer think? I think that if we're frugal, we kin make a few days on this. Let's go and we kin get some good shut eye in that ol' drain culvert. I think we have a couple more weeks thar before we start getting some fall rains and the river fills up again, so we'd best enjoy it fer now!"

Sam was happy to leave the corner, as long as one of their destinations involved food. The pair first stopped at the Liquor Mart, priorities being what they were, for Ernest to stock up on the Red Dawg. He bought a larger bottle, since they were flush for cash, and he wanted to be prepared when he needed an extra swig. Then, they stopped by the Grocery Stop for some solid food. Sam waited outside while Ernest went in to shop. Per his normal process, Ernest came out with both a bag of purchased items and a jacket full of items acquired through his five-finger-discount process.

"After all this, I still have four dollars left if we have an 'mergency. Ah'm likin' to plan ahead if I kin." Ernest explained.

The pair munched on pepperoni slices, one of Sam's favorites, as they walked back toward the river. They backtracked to the south along the east trail, but decided to cross the river on the Twenty Third Street Bridge instead of the walking bridge, since they both wanted to check in on the tent village where Rosine, Edwin and Gerald were living. The Twenty Third Street Bridge was primarily intended as an automobile bridge, however it did have a sidewalk across the span, protected from the main traffic area by a concrete wall. Sam and Ernest had to climb an inclined walkway, rising about three stories, to get from the river bank to the bridge itself. Once on top, they both stopped and looked down at the clearing to catch a glimpse of the tent village.

They both spotted it quickly. "I can't believe how yer can see them tents so easy if yer know what ter look fer. That old Gerald is a bastard, but I hopes Edwin and Rosine are getting' along fer themselves."

Sam paused for a moment by the light post where Edwin had pirated the electric run for the tent village. Ernest took notice as well, saying, "Will yer looky there! The 'lectric comp'ny must er found Edwin's wires there, unhooked 'em, and locked that pole back down. I wonder what they're goin' ter do for heat this winter. Edwin's damned smart. Ah'm sure they'll figger sompn out to keep warm."

Ernest gave a hollow wave to the tent village and the pair trudged across the bridge. The sidewalk was uncomfortably close to the four lanes of traffic passing across the bridge. The larger cars and trucks stirred up enough wind to push Sam and Ernest as they passed, but the concrete wall gave them some feeling of safety. Like the walking bridge, joggers and bikers passed by the two in relatively close quarters across the half-mile span. Then, when the trail widened on the west side again, the pair was given a wider berth by passers-by.

The trail wound beneath the west side of the bridge and made its way to parallel the river. Sam and Ernest continued along, turning south to head back to their culvert.

"Yer know, Sam, we're gonna have ter find sompn else for the winter. That ol' culvert is good for another week 'er two 'er three, but she'll be under water soon enough. Let's us start explorin' our options tomorrer. We'll head uptown to see what we kin find." Ernest was pleased with his responsible and proactive approach to the coming winter, and felt himself to be somewhat parental in that respect.

"Well, how 'bout that ol' buggy!" Ernest exclaimed, pointing out a stray shopping cart turned on its side and crammed squarely into the scrub brush between the trail and the river. "That ol' cart may be right helpful fer us. Let's go check 'er out!"

The rusty cart had obviously not been in service at any reputable grocery store for a long while. It was built entirely from metal, both the frame and basket, unlike the more modern carts with their plastic baskets. Ernest, carefully avoiding the briars and what appeared to be some poison ivy, dragged the relic from the rough ground and up onto the trail, grinning widely as he righted it and walked around to admire his find.

"We'll take this back to our culvert fer a quick escape vehicle if that there water rises. We can pack our gear up right fast, and use this here cart to move on out. This must be our lucky day!"

Sam was not so convinced. The cart was not only rusty; the side that had been buried in the briars was covered with mud and filth. The basket was bent inward around the corners, and the wheels were worn down and broken in places, so it was questionable if they would really roll at all. Sam had observed Ernest to have consistently good ideas and so wasn't ready to argue or complain about his plan for this dirty chunk of metal.

Ernest proudly pushed his new toy down the trail, with the rough wheels bouncing across the asphalt and squealing loudly as they spun on their axles for the first time in what had to be months. Joggers and bikers who even before the acquisition of the shopping cart would have given Sam and Ernest plenty of room to pass, went completely off the trail and onto the grass to let the pair by. Some of the dirt and filth rattled off the basket as it dried in the sun and vibrated across the pavement, so, by the time the pair reached the fence by the refinery, the cart didn't look quite so hideous. Still, Sam wondered if Ernest wouldn't be better off simply carrying his belongings.

When they came to the break in the fence, Ernest looked up and down the trail to make sure no one was watching, then pushed the cart down the hill a few yards and laid it on its side in the tall grass.

"Thar!" he said, "Nobody'll see 'er layin' thar. She'll be thar when we need 'er."

Mission accomplished, the pair slipped through the fence and made their way to the culvert. Sleep came easily, thanks to a full day of activity and comfortably full bellies.

9. Winter Rain

Like most mornings over the past week, Sam awoke to a flash of light followed a few seconds later by a crack of thunder that he could feel as well as hear. He couldn't see the sun through the thick clouds and sheets of rain, but he could tell that day was breaking because of the twilight color to the east. He could also tell that day was breaking because, even over Ernest's snores, he could hear the sound of the cars on Riverside Drive across the now-flowing Arkansas River. He stood and stretched, yawning with his mouth open widely as he felt the stretching push fresh blood into his muscles. He then stepped around his snoring friend to get a look at the river.

The middle part of the culvert tube now housed a musty odor and had a small stream of water running down it, presumably seeping through the earth into the pipe above and draining down. The little stream didn't cause much of a problem unless Sam or Ernest rolled over in their sleep, giving them an abrupt and cold awakening. The corps' high-water sirens had been sounding for the past several days, but the rains had been falling so consistently that there really hadn't been a good opportunity for the pair to get out and move without a thorough soaking. So, they watched the rain, watched the river rise, rationed their food, and waited. The river's waters, which were at least ten feet from the culvert yesterday, had now risen almost to the edge of the culvert's opening. It would be time to leave soon, even if it meant getting out in the heavy rain.

Sam quietly nudged Ernest, working to wake him gently and avoid a soggy roll into the stream at the bottom of the culvert. However, as usual, Ernest woke with a start, wailing in anguish "Shondra Lee, I'm right here. I'll work really hard, I really will, …. Aw, damn! Sorry 'bout that Sam, I was jest thinkin' about mah Shondra Lee and mah family. I sure miss 'em. I sure wish I wasn't so bad fer 'em. If I could get responsible... If I could get free o' that old Red Dawg, I might could go back."

Sam understood Ernest's sentiment, but also understood that there wasn't much he could do for his friend in that regard.

"Yer a good buddy, thar Sam," Ernest continued as he stood to look out of the culvert between the bars of the grate. "It looks like we'll have ter leave terday. I ain't real excited 'bout trudgin' off in that thar mud, but that water's about up ter our porch so I s'pose its time ter go. It looks like yer ready ter head out. Let me wake up a bit, then let's load up the cart and go. We'll head uptown to that old concrete ramp in the Civic Center parkin' garage for a stretch. It's a busy place, so we prob'ly won't be able to stay put thar fer the whole winter, but it'll do us jus' fine for a place 'er transition."

Sam stretched again, not sure whether to smile at the opportunity for a new adventure or to frown at the prospect of leaving this shelter for the long walk through the rain to the covered parking structure they had identified a few weeks ago. The space they found beneath a concrete entrance ramp would make a warm and dry, if somewhat cramped shelter for the pair. The only real drawback was that the parking garage was quite busy, and there would be times during the day where they wouldn't be able to come or go without the risk of being discovered.

Once fully awake, Ernest scampered around the culvert, preparing for a permanent departure. He crammed the belongings worth taking into his blanket roll, then stuffed the blanket roll into the remnants of a plastic garbage bag. He then put his head through a hole in another garbage bag, fashioning it as a poncho, and helped Sam do the same. Sam felt it was uncomfortable to wear the plastic bag and complained about it, but Ernest assured him that he would be happy he had it once he was in the rain.

Now properly packed, the pair said a quick goodbye to the culvert, their home for more than a month, and sloshed out into the rain. Ernest slipped through the muddy ground, lugging the rolled blanket and supplies behind him in a Santa-like way. Sam followed closely, watching Ernest's habitual limp. As usual, Sam was much more sure-footed. When they passed through the fence, forcing the blanket roll through the narrow passage, they found the shopping cart on its side in the weeds. Ernest righted the cart, tossed the blanket roll into the muddy basket, and the two made their way north on the river trail toward downtown.

Just like before, the shopping cart's worn wheels squealed and wailed as they started down the path. However, as the rain water worked its way into and around the axles, they quieted dramatically. Sam walked slowly beside Ernest and watched the rain fall around him. As Ernest had predicted, Sam was now pleased to be covered up in the plastic bag, as his exposed feet were now soaked to the skin and felt very cold. His yellow coat, dry beneath the cover of the garbage bag, kept the rest of him warm and comfortable.

Sam was mesmerized, watching the raindrops as he walked. If he watched at a distance, they appeared as streaks across the air. If he looked straight up, they would occasionally fall directly in his eyes. If he looked down, he could find endless patterns formed by the splashing of the water. The drops that fell directly down appeared to bounce in the thin film of water covering the trail. A small circle would form as they hit, then the circle was immediately consumed by the water around it as a smaller droplet flew upward. The drops that fell on his plastic bag "poncho" flattened out and rolled over his shoulders, eventually falling to the trail, looking the same as a drop that fell directly from the sky. Some drops were bigger than others, causing larger circles that lasted a bit longer. The larger drops also pounded the grass and other plants along the side of the trail. Sam found it interesting that the same water that appeared to damage the plants with the impact of the rain would cause them to turn greener with a fresh supply of life as it soaked into the ground.

The smell of the rain was also very interesting. Sam loved the smell of the air when the rain first started. He thought that the rain itself might bring the odor from the cloudy sky. Or, maybe the rain caused the earth and plants on which it fell to produce the new odor. He decided that, as long as he enjoyed it, the reason didn't matter. He also found that once the rain had established itself, the strength of the smell subsided. However, the smell did stay, just ever so faint.

As a simple being, Sam always found beauty in the sights and smells around him. He didn't notice Ernest watching him enjoy the scene.

"Walkin' in the rain ain't so bad if yer have a garbage bag ter keep yer dry!" he chuckled to Sam. "When yer not cold and miserable, it's right pleasant. I'm glad yer appreciate it terday. We have a bit of a stroll ahead of us, but we'll be awl right. Also, when the weather's like this, we'll not have anybody botherin' us on ther way. It aurt to be a peaceful walk fer us."

The pair crossed on the Twenty Third Street Bridge so they wouldn't have to travel south to the walking bridge only to head back north to downtown. On this rainy day there were no joggers or bikers to pass close to them on the sidewalk. The rain seemed to be coming down harder on the bridge, but it was really just spray from cars passing them. They did take a moment to look over onto the tent village in the clearing on the east side. Not surprisingly, they saw no activity outside the tents. However, they both knew that Edwin, Rosine and Gerald were likely warm and dry inside. Upon observing that the power wires were still disconnected from the street lamp and that the lamp's base was still shut tightly, Ernest chuckled to Sam, "I wonder if ol' Edwin's noticed that there ain't no 'lectricity comin' through ter 'em now? He'd best figger it out quick, lest they get a serious chill when winter really arrives."

Traveling up Denver Avenue, Ernest grunted and strained to push the old shopping cart up the steep hill. The elevation rose more than three hundred feet up out of the river basin in the course of only a quarter mile, making the climb a test even for a strong runner or an automobile. His feet slipped occasionally as the cart wheels hit the cracks in the sidewalk, but he continued his methodical push up the hill. Once they passed the Grocery Stop and were into the main part of downtown, the street began to level out.

On a clear day, the sidewalks would have been crowded with people. Joggers and business people as well as other *rough sleepers* would be moving about the streets. The wet and stormy weather, however, had chased all but the hardiest and most desperate few out of the elements and into whatever shelter could be found. The downtown streets and sidewalks were largely deserted.

Sam did notice a few *rough sleepers* huddled in a covered bus stop. They didn't make eye contact, nod, wave or otherwise acknowledge Sam or Ernest. As a result, the pair didn't stop to converse. Ernest provided a quiet background monolog for Sam as they passed by: "Yer never knows what ter expect from summon livin' out here. Some folks is right fine, but others is plumb crazy. Sum of 'em that ain't crazy on their own has to fight thar demons like I does. Yer never knows if they was on the hooch er on the meth er sniffin' up on some toilet cleaner. And that can make some folks right mean and dangerous. I think if we don't know 'em, we're best to steer clear of 'em." Sam was happy to keep his distance as well.

While the plastic bag did keep him dry, Sam felt a bit constrained in his movements, and therefore a bit more vulnerable to the threats around him. This made him uncomfortable during the walk. However, he was confident that he would be even more uncomfortable if he was getting soaked to the bone without the cover of the plastic bag.

The glistening high-rise apartments on South Denver Avenue gave way to the crumbling remnants of the old YMCA building as they continued their walk into downtown. The YMCA building, which had once served as shelter and temporary home to many *rough sleepers*, had been abandoned in favor of a facility catering more to the downtown business professional than to someone down on his luck. The building was no longer used, and was beginning to deteriorate. Sam and Ernest had given the building a very close look, searching for opportunities to enter undetected and possibly make a winter home in one of the offices or handball courts. Unfortunately, the building's new owners had chosen to invest heavily in solid doors and locks which successfully prevented temporary habitation by *rough sleepers*.

The two walked on until they turned into the Civic Center complex, and Ernest looked quickly up and down the street. Seeing no obvious onlookers, he abruptly steered the cart into a concrete stairwell leading down to the parking garage.

"Jump right in here, Sam, b'fore summon sees yer lookin' to get in. We sure don't want ter be follered by summon, whether they're lookin' for shelter or lookin' to keep folks like us out," Ernest advised. "Gettin' in an' outter here is gonna be the tricky part fer us."

Ernest bounced the cart down the damp stairs on its rear wheels, one stair at a time, with the cart groaning each time it hit the next stair down. Two flights down, he turned out of the stairwell and darted across the parking lot and then crouched down, with Sam, himself and the cart parked between a Hummer and a minivan.

"Looky up at them shiny balls on the ceilin', thar Sam," Ernest pointed through the tinted windows of the minivan. "Them are cam'ras and yer never know whether the s'curity men are watchin'. When we're comin' or goin', we have ter watch to stay away from whar them balls can see us. If them s'curity men see us travelin' round down here, they'll come down and find us right quick, and we'll be lookin' fer a new place before yer know it."

Ernest could see that Sam understood the need to be quick and stealthy when making his way around the parking garage.

"From here, we're gonna head out to the driveway, turn right, then get ter the entrance ramp from the street right quick, and go under it. Once we're under, we're in the clear. Got it?" Ernest asked. "It'll be jist like it was when we was casin' the place a while back."

Sam confirmed, and the two jumped out and walked quickly up to the entrance ramp. Sam remembered the place now. They had checked it out a few weeks ago, knowing that the culvert wouldn't do once the rains started. The entrance ramp was a slab of concrete that bridged the street level with the garage level about four feet below it. In doing so, it formed a wedge of space below it, making a solid, though vertically constrained, living area for the two. It was almost as good as the old bridge on Cincinnati! The cart would just barely fit under the slab at its tallest point, and both Sam and Ernest had to duck to enter. They wasted no time getting under and out of sight, then sat down with their backs to the flat wall at the highest spot and smiled at each other while catching their breath.

"This'll work, won't it, Sam!" Ernest was pleased and knew that Sam was as well. It might have looked roomier a few weeks ago, but even as cramped as it was, being inside here and out of the wind and rain was perfect for now. Sam also noticed that it was warmer under the ramp than it had been outside. That would be a huge comfort as the winter cold set in.

Ernest removed his trash-bag poncho, and Sam shook out of his. Sam stretched, happy to be out of the bag, but knowing that the discomfort was worthwhile in the rain.

They stacked the bags in the shopping cart and then went about spreading blankets in the dry areas for places to sit and sleep. They had to push away the typical trash, gravel and candy wrappers, along with liquor bottles and cigarette butts, but, it was worth the effort to have a comfortable place to stay. They stacked the trash toward the front of the ramp where the ceiling was too low to be comfortable; they didn't want to draw attention to the space by creating a trash heap outside in the parking garage. As they did so, Sam noticed some movement in the far corner of the covered area and immediately alerted Ernest.

"What the hell do yer s'pose is hidin' back thar? I'll bet its some varmit, and it probably ain't really happy that we're takin' over the place. What's worse is that I think that hole we came in from is the only way outter here, so that damned varmit is gonna have ter go past us to get away. Dammit, it's always sompn, ain't it?" Ernest shook his head, then rubbed his chin with his hand, saying, "Awl right, I don't want ter go out and wait fer him ter leave, and he won't try ter leave until he knows he kin make it through. So, we need ter give him some space ter get past us. Let's us take our stuff ter that end so he'll have a place ter run out, then we'll start pokin' at him with sticks and gravel 'til he gets tar'd of it and heads out. I jist sure wish I could tell what that damned thing is. I sure hope it ain't no skunk again. I kin handle a 'coon er a possum, but I sure don't want to see no skunk again. I bet yer've had yer fill of 'em too, ain't yer?" Ernest chuckled at the thought of Sam's encounter with the skunk at the river. Sam did not.

They moved to give the creature a clear escape route out of the shelter, and then Ernest began throwing gravel and bottles in its direction. He could tell when he hit something, as it rustled more. However, it didn't move quickly and didn't start to bark or growl or make any menacing noises. They eventually ran out of trash and gravel to throw, still without the creature moving from its place.

"Well, Sam, I guess we'll have a roommate fer a bit. I'm just gonna keep an eye out fer him. He'll need ter git somptn ter eat sooner or later. We jes gotta make sure he don't try ter make a meal from us!" Ernest smiled, adding, "Aw, I'm jist kiddin'. Ain't nothing that could stay under here that could make a meal outter us. I'm sure he's more skeered of us than we are of him. We'll jist have ter let 'em be fer now."

The two heard an occasional rustle from the corner off and on through the remainder of the day, but never did see the creature move. Sam crawled closer to it to get a better look, but it appeared to be snuggled in under clothing and blankets and he couldn't get a good look. He did notice that the creature had a foul, but familiar odor, and like Ernest, Sam hoped that it was not a skunk. The pair napped through the afternoon, always keeping one eye toward the creature, but never seeing it move.

As the air darkened with evening approaching, the downtown workers who parked in the Civic Center garage began their orderly exit. Sam could hear the click-click of footsteps as they crossed the pavement, and he made a mental game of guessing the size and gender of the walker before sticking his nose out around the edge of the ramp to see if he had guessed right. He could easily tell a woman in high-heels or a man in leather loafers, but athletic shoes were extremely hard to guess. Sam was intrigued by the echoes caused by the drivers slamming their car doors closed. He would hear each sound twice: clunk-*clunk*! The second sound was always louder. Again, he sneaked a look outside the ramp to watch the gentleman driving the

Hummer slam his door – hearing one at the same time he saw it close and then hearing the echo a moment later. The noise of the car engines added a third dimension to the racket, and between the clicking of heels, the slamming of doors and the rumbling of the engines, the once-quiet garage now had a consistent low din to it.

"Don't yer worry none, Sam," Ernest counseled, "this'll go on fer a while in the mornin' and in the evenin' an' then she'll quiet down just like she wuz. As winter sets in, we'll 'preciate them noisy engines, since they'll warm this here garage up a bit with their comin' and goin'. "

Sam had no comment, as the racket continued its crescendo to the point that he could barely hear Ernest.

"Damn if it ain't pretty loud right now, though!" Ernest finished the thought, having to yell over the noise of the cars.

The noise of the cars also appeared to be having an effect on the creature hiding in the corner as well. Sam noticed some movement, and stared intently at it, trying to determine what it was and if it posed any danger to himself or Ernest. The wads of clothing and blankets shuffled around, making him wonder if a mother raccoon had made her nest there, or maybe a street cat or stray dog. Again, he hoped it wasn't another skunk. The image and pain of that creature was permanently imprinted on his memory.

The activity and noise subsided after a while, as Ernest had predicted. Still, now and then a straggler would walk through to their car with a click-clack of heels or a shuffle of loafers, so Sam went back to his mental game of working to identify the person based on their sounds. The overall noise of the evening rush, however, had certainly awoken the creature in the corner, as it was starting to rustle around more and grunt and move.

"It must be a momma 'coon," Ernest conjectured, "'cause it's wakin' up fer the evenin'. Them 'coons mostly stays up at night. If it's a momma, we have a problem on our hands – them damned things is plain ol' mean and she ain't likely ter wanna give up her place. We have ter keep a close eye on that as she starts ter wake up. Dammit, that's jist some bad luck fer us. I ain't gonna go cross-ways with no momma 'coon."

There was more rustling and movement from the corner, and some of the blankets folded open. Sam inched toward the creature, hoping to catch a glimpse, but still could not see what was inside the nest of clothing. The unfolding of the blankets did release more of the pungent and familiar odor, however, which gave Sam pause. He instinctively backed away from the creature, the hair on the back of his neck standing on end with a sense of danger.

Ernest saw Sam's retreat, "What der yer smell thar? Damn, I hope it ain't no skunk. I think that would be worse'n a damn 'coon!"

Sam searched his mind. Where had he smelled that odor? Why did it make him nervous?

"Ah'm glad that thang didn't spray us while we were throwin' rocks at it earlier. It would ruin us and this here place."

The creature moved again, and the blanket fell open even more, revealing a grimy hand and arm of a man. The arm reached around, and began to scratch inside the blanket, and then peeled the blanket back revealing the rest of the creature, and a dangerously familiar human face. Sam now understood the chemical smell, and realized why it made his hair stand on the back of his neck.

"Chris, yer damned meth head! Yer best wake yerself up and git on yer way. Yer stole our spot under the bridge, now it's a time fer a little payback, yer bastard!" Ernest was visibly relieved that the creature wasn't a mother raccoon or skunk, but he also understood the danger Chris presented. Not only could Chris injure Ernest or Sam under the ramp, he could also give their home away to a security guard in the garage or to his other meth-head friends.

"Shut up, you old drunk. I'm going to come kick both of your asses, then I'm going to drag you into the street where you'll be picked up by the po-lice. I'll never have to mess with you sorry sons of bitches again." Chris stumbled and swayed as he tried to stoop over to walk toward the pair.

The chemical stink of the meth on Chris was now overwhelming, making Sam a bit nauseous. The effects of the meth on Chris' wretched body, even over just a few months since Sam and Ernest had last seen him, were amazing. When they had first met, Chris appeared to be aged beyond his actual years, and his teeth were small, yellow nubs. Now, only a few teeth remained and his skin was scratched and torn almost everywhere it was exposed by his tattered clothing.

Ernest was having none of Chris' threat. "Yer ain't gonna do nothin' of the sort. Them drugs has wasted yer away. Yer hair is fallin' out in clumps, and yer so thin that I kin see yer joints pokin' out all around. Look at yer torn-up arm thar! I kin put my thumb and pinky around that, and I'll prob'ly snap yer like a chicken wing! Yer ain't gonna cause damage to anyone in that condition."

"I may be a bit under-nourished, but my "friend" here is going to help out a bit," Chris retorted as he swung a heavy, wooden baseball bat, aiming directly at Sam's head.

Sam, agile, even in the cramped space, darted back, and the bat swished harmlessly by. The momentum of the swing, however, wracked Chris' arm into a concrete support post, causing him to scream out in pain as blood streamed down the post and his arm.

"I'll get you now, you som' bitch. You may be quick, but there isn't that much space to move around!" Chris took another swing at Sam with the bat.

Sam dodged again, and then lunged at Chris, pushing him down onto his side with his head smashing against another of the support posts. Chris was visibly dazed, and now bleeding freely from both his arm and his head.

He scrambled to his feet, and growled, "That's it! I've been keeping this place to myself, and haven't told the others about it. But with you two bastards here, I'm going to go chat it up with my crew. They'll appreciate this like they appreciated our space under the bridge, and they'll be back with me to take you two on. I hope you sleep well in here tonight, 'cause it's going to be your last night here!"

Sam and Ernest were both severely disappointed, knowing that they could easily press Chris out the door, but that they had no chance of defending their space against a number of the meth heads. Just like their great shelter beneath the Cincinnati street bridge, they would be kicked out. They would have to wander the now cold streets, working to find another suitable shelter. For Sam, within moments the disappointment turned to sadness, then the sadness turned to despair, then the despair turned to anger, then the anger turned to rage, then the rage turned to action. With fire in his eyes, he lunged at Chris again. Again, he knocked him to the floor, and like the squirrels by the river he was ready to jump on Chris and break his fragile neck. But before he could make the final pounce, Ernest moved faster than Sam had ever seen him move. Ernest caught Sam by the shoulder and held him back, allowing Sam to only stare at the fragile shell of a man. Sam loved to see the fear in Chris' bloodshot eyes. The fear he saw made Sam smile inside, knowing that he could take Chris down any time he wanted. Still, Ernest held him back. Chris scooted and scrambled toward to the opening to the garage, taking his bat and whatever blankets he could carry.

Once out from under the ramp, he stood and began running for the stairwell, then out to the street. Ernest released Sam, and they both followed Chris.

The cold rain was still falling in the darkness, but they could see Chris look back as he ran toward the five lanes of busy rush hour traffic. "I'll be back with more, you som' bitches! Just like the bridge, we'll be back, and you'd better be gone!" Chris sprinted ahead toward Boston Avenue.

In the distance below the street lights, they could see Chris dodge through the first lane of traffic. He still held his bat in one hand and was dragging his blankets behind him with the other. They then watched a car in the second lane swerve to miss him, colliding with another car in the process. The mangled cars slid along the rain-soaked street, coming to rest on the adjacent sidewalk. As they did, a small delivery van struck Chris squarely, sending him up onto the windshield, carrying him along for a split second. As the driver stood on the brakes, Chris dropped off the front of the van and rolled along the street. He came to rest in a crumpled mess where the asphalt of the street met the concrete curb of the sidewalk.

"Well, I guess he ain't gonna tell his friends about us ternight. I don't wish evil on nobody, but I think that bastard got what he deserved. Let's go see how this whole thang plays out."

They went back below to put on their garbage bag ponchos, and quietly walked to the scene of the crash. By the time they arrived, the fire department trucks had arrived, and the police were diverting traffic around the three lanes involved in the crash. Even with the cold rain, many *rough sleepers* were observing the scene. The collision and subsequent cleanup provided a little excitement on the street for the evening. They could see a lump of clothing and flesh where Chris had landed. His limbs were contorted in unnatural positions. The paramedics worked around Chris for a while, and eventually loaded him onto a gurney. As they raised him into the ambulance, Sam could see that Chris' face was covered with a sheet.

"Well, yer knows what that means, don'cher?" Ernest nodded at the covered body on the gurney. "Ol' Chris has run his course. I think that ol' meth is really what did him in. That delivery van that hit him was just finishing things off. He'd be dead soon one way 'er another. That damned old van just took him home. It's good it was quick."

"Let's find our way back under the ramp fer the night. It's a lot warmer there. Jest be careful we ain't follered. We don't need no more comp'ny ternight."

The anonymous pair quietly walked back to their shelter, taking care to look around them before darting under the ramp. While Sam was shocked to see Chris' death, he was relieved that Chris would not be giving their shelter away to the rest of the meth heads. Especially now with the "creature" gone, Sam felt this would be an excellent new home and he hoped to spend the rest of the winter there.

Once back under the ramp, Ernest and Sam arranged pallets from their blankets and found the tallest area, the one against the concrete wall, to be the most comfortable. That area still held the warmth of the ground, and was high enough for them both to walk, even if somewhat bent over. Ernest grumbled if he had to crawl on his hands and knees in a more confined space. "Mah knees ain't what they used ter be when I was younger. They make funny noises when I bend 'em, and the pain in 'em gives me fits. I don't need to be spendin' a lot of time on mah knees," he would say.

They arranged the squeaky shopping cart along the entrance to the area under the ramp. It was not visible from above, but the noise of it's movement would alert them if someone decided to pay a visit beneath the ramp.

After getting comfortable, Ernest found his bottle of Red Dawg and began his regular lament. "Yer know, Sam, mah wife, Shondra Lee, she kept tellin' me that I cain't take care of nothin'. Not even mahself. She said I cain't stay away from the Red Dawg long enough to hold down a job, an' I cain't be 'sponsible enough to stay with them kids." He took a long draw on the bottle. "But, yer know, I'm a long sight better off 'n that old Chris. I knows enough to stay away from that meth. I knows enough to stay away from that heroin, and I kin stay away from this here Red Dawg if I give it a try."

With that, Sam worked to pull the bottle away from Ernest's grasp. First a light tug, then a heavier one, until Ernest firmed up. "Not so fast there, yer sunofergun, not so fast. I'll decide when its time fer me ter let go. It ain't fer yer to decide when. I'll decide when I'm good 'n ready. And ternight ain't the night."

Sam was disappointed that tonight wasn't the night for Ernest to give up the bottle. Sam had felt the irony of Ernest's rant at Chris. In the time Sam had known Ernest, he had seen how the Red Dawg was taking his life away, a little bit at a time. The effects were not as pronounced as those of the meth. The teeth that Ernest had lost were from trauma and neglect as opposed to the chemicals, and the malnourishment and frailty of his body was more from an inconsistent diet than his inability to metabolize the food. Nonetheless, the alcohol binges took their toll. Each binge slowed Ernest just a bit. Each binge made him look and act just that much older. Each binge took him farther from his wife and family.

Despite those sad thoughts spinning through his head, Sam slept well that night. He didn't have to listen for the sound of the Corps of Engineers' sirens, and he didn't worry about the meth addicts taking over their shelter. He awoke to the rhythmic sounds of car tires entering the garage and rolling down their concrete roof, followed by echoing slams of doors and the click-clack of heels and loafers. Another work day was starting for the good citizens who parked in the Civic Center garage.

10. Trapped

Sam shared Ernest's desire to not be found in this shelter, and so was happy to stay under the ramp as the cacophony of the morning rush gave way to an isolated car squeaking down the ramp or a solitary set of loafers going tap-tap across the concrete floor of the parking garage. He did feel a little cramped, having to stay low and quiet when the day started, but that was a minor inconvenience compared to scouting out a new dwelling.

Having been confined to the culvert by the refinery for almost a week without a resupply, both food and money were running low. Between the two, they had fifty-three cents and four slices of American cheese "product." Ernest swore that the fake American cheese was superior to the real thing. "I'll tell yer, this here cheese stuff will last 'til the next ice age! I don't know what they put in this stuff, but ah'm glad they invented it. I don't care if it ain't one hunred percent real. It tastes fine, and saves a long time in mah carry bag." Sam wasn't as enthusiastic about the imitation cheese as Ernest. While it looked like a slice of cheese, the odor wasn't quite right. Odor or not, however, he could tolerate it, especially when rations were running low.

In the early afternoon, as Sam gulped down the last of the American cheese product, Ernest motioned for him to come along out into the world to help him rustle up some food or some money or both.

"C'mon, there Sam, let's go git us somp'n to eat. I ain't hungry now, but I will be soon enough. It ain't real cold, but it's still rainin' a little, so we'll look good and pathetic out there. We kin stay close by ter the steam pipe vents, an' mebbie stay a little warmer yet. Let's git us enough for a trip to the Grocery Stop and a bottle o' Red Dawg! That'll make mah day, fer sure!"

Leaving their garbage bag ponchos behind, the two ducked out from under the ramp, nonchalantly walked across the dusty floor, and quietly navigated between the larger vehicles in the parking garage. They eventually found their way to the concrete steps leading up to Seventh Street. Sam's nose caught an odd scent in the stairwell, and looked up to see some designs on the wall that had been freshly spray painted.

"Them damned graffiti kids. They ain't got nuthin' better ter do than ter steal some paint and sign their names on the walls. Ah'm surprised they know how ter spell their names, the bastards. They're just like damned dogs, pissin' on a far hydrant er a light pole ter mark their territory. This sort o' crap'll bring the secur'ty man around more, which you an' me sure don't need."

Aside from Ernest's swearing, there wasn't much to be done about the graffiti, so they pressed ahead to the top of the stairs. Both the street and the sidewalk were quiet with the grey mid-winter Oklahoma sky casting a dreary tint to the day. The downtown trees had lost their leaves long ago, and though they were only dormant for the winter, they carried a lifeless look. While it wasn't exactly raining, a cold mist kept pedestrians off the street, and kept most cars parked in their underground garages and surface lots until the work day was over. Despite the desolation, Ernest was optimistic, "Don't worry none. Once the quittin' bell rings for these folk, the streets will be busy enough. Most of 'em drive in from twenty miles out, so they'll be in one big hurry to git themselves home. These here lights on Boulder Ave'nue will stop 'em long enough for us to look needy and deserving, and fer them to feel guilty about sittin' on their heated leather seats with the climate control blowin' warm and dry in their face. We'll do fine at quittin' time! 'Til then, let's go check out the Dumpster behind the Route 66 Lodge to see if anything fresh is cookin'. I knows them uptown hotels is a better bet, but it's a long sight off, an' I wants to be back here in time to get us some Red Dawg money when rush hour starts!"

Sam complied, though he would have much preferred the gourmet leftovers of the uptown hotels to the more pedestrian fare at the Route 66. The restaurant at the Route 66 Lodge had a fairly broad menu, but seemed to serve almost exclusively hamburgers and turkey sandwiches. The patrons there appeared to eat more thoroughly than those uptown, and frequently would leave a little bread but rarely any of the turkey or beef. Sam was a bit put out, knowing that they could have food – and good food at that – behind his favorite uptown hotels, but they were skipping that to make sure they could panhandle for Red Dawg money. Sam didn't like the fact that Ernest was a slave to the bottle, and liked it even less when he was inconvenienced by Ernest's habit.

The Dumpster in the alley behind the Route 66 Lodge was propped open with black garbage bags, and it looked as though the trash pickup would need to happen soon to keep the bags from having to be piled outside. The alley was narrow, with an aged and bumpy brick covering. There was just enough space for a garbage truck to pull in to empty the trash bin on its appointed days. The cold, damp weather appeared to be keeping any other interested *rough sleepers* from competing for the best morsels on this day, so Sam and Ernest found themselves alone in the alley. Employees of the Route 66 also appeared to be spending their time inside, as opposed to sneaking smokes in the alley, again likely because of the uncomfortable weather. With no competition and no workers to interfere, Ernest casually picked out the top bag. He expected it to have the freshest leftovers, and he was not disappointed.

"Looky here, Sam!" Ernest spoke as though he was opening cherished gifts on Christmas morning. "Here's half a hamburger with the patty still there! An' here's the fries to go with 'er. Let's us take this one bag over yonder there and just take our time with 'er instead of worryin' about sommun else commin' around. What der ya say?"

Sam was like-minded, and so he followed Ernest down the alley a few hundred feet where they ducked into a recessed doorway which offered some shelter to stay out of the mist and enjoy the best parts of their meal. Ernest wobbled as he carried the heavy bag, but wore a smile as he did. When they were settled, Ernest reopened the bag and tossed the hamburger and fries over to Sam. As Sam started the hamburger, Ernest pulled part of a fried fish patty from the bag.

"I usually don't think it's a good idear to eat the fish from the Route 66 Lodge, but since it's still warm, I think I'll make an exception. And, even better, look here there's some tartar sauce. This here's a plain ol' feast fer us!"

Sam thoroughly enjoyed his half-hamburger as Ernest devoured the fish, effectively slathering it in the tartar sauce. Sam was happy to concede the fish to Ernest. He would eat it if nothing else was available, but it wasn't his first choice.

When the pair had eaten their fill, Ernest threw the bag back into the nearest Dumpster, since Ernest felt that the lodge was less likely to complain about *rough sleepers* if they didn't leave a big mess. They then sauntered up the alley to the opposite end. As they passed another recessed doorway, much like the one they had just used as an al fresco café, Sam saw the shell of a sleeping man curled up under a sweatshirt and a tattered blanket.

Sam stopped to study the scene. The man was older than he or Ernest, but he wasn't old by most standards. He was weather-worn, with tough leathery skin on his hands and parts of his face that were not covered. He carried a stench of cheap grain alcohol mixed with the ammonia-like odor that could only be explained through a combination of fermented perspiration, vomit and urine. He had obviously wet himself in his drunken binge, and was not aware enough or concerned enough to clean himself. Sam could see the man's stomach rise and fall as he worked to push air in and out of his lungs. The effort he put forth in that activity seemed to tire him more with each breath. It was a depressing sight, indeed. More so for Sam, in that he could see how with each bottle of Red Dawg Ernest was growing closer to living a life like the one he saw before him.

Ernest, however, wouldn't admit that he made the connection. "Let's go, Sam," he chided. "There ain't nuthin' ter see here. That ol' feller is just more down on his luck than we are. Just look at his red nose and the wrinkles across his forehead. He ain't been doin' so well out here, and he ain't gonna make it much longer. He even looks too pathetic to be a good 'handler. He jist ain't gonna make it much longer out here. The poor bastard. Let's go."

Beyond the words, though, Sam understood why Ernest didn't want to stay and look at the old man. He wouldn't admit it to Sam and he wouldn't admit it to himself, but Ernest knew that his fate and the fate of the man in the doorway could be one and the same. Ernest knew that there was little productive life left for the man in the doorway. Even when he was lucid, he would be constantly in a search to fill his alcohol habit. He would forsake food and cleanliness and other necessities of life to feed his demon. The demon that had taken his brain would eventually take his liver and his life as well.

The pair found their way back to Boulder Avenue, and then followed it south to Seventh Street, where the timed light would hold up the most traffic as the rush hour started.

"This here will be our best bet fer some handlin'," Ernest said as he spread a blanket on the grate over the steam pipes. "Let's have a seat here fer a bit. This ol' blanket'll make this grate a bit more bearable to sit on. Once we have a lineup on the street, we kin start farmin' it. If this here mist will keep up, but not turn ter rain, we'll be pretty comf'table but still look wet and needy. This here night will be perfect!"

Sam sat with Ernest, enjoying the warmth coming through the blanket from the steam pipes below the grate. The sidewalks were growing busy with workers leaving to find their cars, and the traffic was building in the street. Yet, even with all the activity and Ernest sitting directly beside him, Sam felt lonely. Aside from Ernest, the people near him on the street would hardly look his way. Those who did, completely avoided eye contact, and hurried past. The drivers on the street, even those waiting at a standstill for the traffic light to change, would not acknowledge his existence. Sam knew that he was there, but he wondered if he was really invisible to the world around him.

A small child, holding his mother's hand as they walked past, gave him hope that he could be seen.

"Momma? What are they doing on that blanket on the sidewalk?" he inquired.

"Ssssh! Just keep walking, Logan. Just leave them alone," his mother whispered.

The child, Logan, stared at Sam and Ernest even if his mother avoided any recognition of the two. Ernest's eyes were closed as he leaned against the building, but Sam stared back. He was enjoying the fact that he could, indeed, be seen by the people around him. He didn't understand why the people appeared to ignore him. He could see them interact with the other passer's by. Some would be engaged in conversation. Others would simply smile at each other, or utter, "Excuse me," as they slipped past each other in packs. But, uniformly, they all ignored Sam and Ernest.

"Awl, right. I think we has enough traffic out there to make it worth our while. Let's have yer sit closer ter the street. Jus stay right there and look sad and hungry and pathetic. I'll pass the hat when the light turns red. It'll be like shootin' fish in a barrel!"

True to the plan, when the light cycled back to red, Ernest made his way out to the cars, five lanes across, waiting impatiently to be let go. He would approach the driver's side and wave a gloved hand. When he caught the drivers attention, he worked to have them lower their window for a conversation. Most would ignore him or motion for him to go away. But, when the driver was too startled to ignore him or too shy to shoo him away, he would ask for a donation while pointing over to Sam who simply sat in the mist working to look needy and pathetic.

Ernest thought they were doing fairly well. "Well, Sam," Ernest provided a quick financial status, "Ah've had twelve cars that would talk ter me in about twenty red lights. That ain't bad. Ah've collected nine dollars and twenty eight cents. If we kin stay at that rate fer another twenty lights, we'll be set fer the day. Yer jus stay there, look needy, and stare at whoever'll talk ter me. That'll shake the change loose, fer sure!"

They actually did better through the next several lights, and Ernest came back to the curb with a big smile on his face. "That last driver looked over at yer sad face and dropped me a fiver! I jus told her that you ain't had nuthin' ter eat fer four days an that's why yer look so scrawny. She was happy ter donate ter the cause! 'Course, I didn't tell her nothin' of the burger yer jus had back at the Route 66 Lodge! We collected more 'n twenty-three dollars ternight. It's too bad we can't do this full-time, er we'd be rich! Let's go git me a new supply o' hooch, and we'll do a run ter the Grocery Stop tomorrer!"

The short walk to the Liquor Mart was slowed by the rush hour traffic. The pair had to wait for the lights at the intersections, instead of crossing the streets midway through the block because the breaks in the traffic were too small to run across. Sam was a little perturbed by this inconvenience, and more so by the fact that they were making the trip only to feed Ernest's Red Dawg habit, and his body language showed his frustration.

"Goin' home will be faster." Ernest sensed Sam's mood, adding, "The traffic is dyin' down already. I knows yer tar'd, but yer knows we couldn't have made our way back under the ramp while all the workers was goin' home anyway. By the time we git back, the garage'll be nice and quiet."

The Liquor Mart was busy with commuters picking up libations for the evening. Sam waited outside the Liquor Mart while Ernest did his shopping.

"Good news, Sam! They was havin' a sale on the Red Dawg ternight! Since they was so cheap, I got two of 'em to stock up! We still have six bucks to go ter the Grocery Stop tomorrer, and yer knows I kin make that go a long way over there." Ernest could tell that Sam was even angrier. It reminded him of how Shondra Lee would react in the last days he spent at home. "C'mon Sam, we'll get some good grub tomorrer. Let's head fer the garage so we can get some good shut-eye."

The streets quieted dramatically as they made their way back toward the garage. By the time they arrived, most of the traffic lights stood alone at the corners with no cars to inconvenience.

The pair found their way to the garage stairwell on Seventh Street, looked around to see no cars in sight, and then hastily ducked in. As they did so, Sam caught the scent of the graffiti paint he had noticed earlier in the day. He thought nothing of it, as the smell had been there as they left the garage. However, smell became stronger and stronger as they continued down the stairs, and Ernest noticed the fresh "artwork" on the wall at the bottom of the stairwell.

"Dammit, those graffiti punks are gettin' bold. That's gonna be a problem fer us, I tell yer." Ernest studied the round, cartoon-like letters on the wall. "Yer'd think they'd at least do some art. Them is just summon's name in some drawed-out letters. What a damned mess. Them graffiti guys is just dogs pissin on the trees. Bastards!"

Ernest shook his head in disgust while he and Sam sprinted across the near-empty garage to the ramp. They were unable to hide from the security cameras by darting between cars, so the best they could do was to minimize their time on-camera. He was still fuming about the graffiti when they ducked under the concrete ramp.

"I can't believe them bastards. They're gonna make the security men start lookin' around more, and they're gonna git way too close ter us. If we see them damned fools, we have ter chase 'em away ourselves, or we're gonna find ourselves without a place ter stay right quick."

Ernest stewed for a while, grumbling about the mess that graffiti painters made on the walls and worrying about the additional scrutiny it would bring. As Sam expected, Ernest eventually transitioned into his typical sad time, lamenting his separation from his family, as he began to nip at the Red Dawg.

"Aw, c'mon Shondra Lee! Puhleeze take me back. I promise that I'll be a good husband, and I'll take care of you and them kids. I'll work real hard, yer'll see! I miss yer so, and I wants ter be with yer and them kids!"

Sam worried that Ernest would attract the attention of someone in the garage, and pushed on him to get his attention. Ernest, however, was not interested in quieting down and took a clumsy swing at Sam. Sam easily dodged

Ernest's fist, but Ernest countered with cruel words founded in his guilt and booze. "Dammit, Sam. This ain't fer you to pass judgment on! If I feel like makin' some noise, I'll do it. I found this here place, and if I get us caught, then that's just the way its gonna go. Yer need me, and yer wouldn't make it without me, so yer just better mind yer own business and say outta mah way!"

Sam felt the sting of the words through the tone of Ernest's voice. This wasn't the first time that Ernest had made thoughtless remarks to Sam. While the words and the tone certainly hurt, Sam knew that they were more an expression of Ernest's hatred of himself than his displeasure with Sam. Sam knew that he and Ernest were a team, and they helped each other out. Their relationship was not simply one-way, and both benefited. In situations like this, when he was full of sorrow and booze, Ernest just didn't see both sides of things.

Sam kept his distance while Ernest drank and cursed his way to sleep. Fortunately, no security guard appeared at the edge of the concrete ramp and no other *rough sleepers* came to see what the commotion was about. Once Ernest was down for the evening, Sam curled up on his pallet, working his way beneath some blankets for some added warmth. Surprisingly, he slept well that night. He woke early in the morning as the lids of a nearby Dumpster banged against a garbage truck during the emptying process. He fell back asleep after the racket, dozing through noise of the morning rush and woke only when the hunger pangs returned to his stomach.

Sam looked over at Ernest. He was still fast asleep, with a little drip of spittle hanging from his lip, snoring relatively quietly. While Ernest didn't look as bad as the man they had seen in the alley the day before, Sam could see him sliding down that slope.

Sam's stomach tugged at him, and while Ernest held the money they had collected the day before, Sam felt hungry enough to go forage for some scraps on his own while Ernest continued to sleep the Red Dawg out of his system. Sam quietly stepped past Ernest and poked his head out from under the concrete ramp. He could see that all the parking spaces were full, confirming his suspicion that he had slept through the morning rush. Yet, there was an odd din of conversation reverberating through the garage, making him uneasy. He silently stepped from beneath the ramp, and slipped behind the first row of cars, making his way toward the conversation. He found the source near the concrete stairway where he and Ernest had entered the garage the previous night – all surrounding the graffiti.

"We're going to have to start watching more closely, gentlemen." Four security guards were listening to an older man in a dark grey suit. "We simply can't afford to keep painting over all this vandalism every time one of these punks decides he wants to write on our walls. I need you guys to keep a keen eye on the cameras and I want at least one of you walking through the garage all night, every night, until these guys either give up or find a better place to deface. Everybody got it?" The security guards all nodded their understanding, and Sam dashed back down the row of cars and under the ramp.

Ernest was coming to life and noticed Sam's harried entrance.

"What's the problem thar, Sam? Yer look like ol' Chris came back from the dead and was chasin' yer through the garage!"

Sam quietly showed Ernest to the edge of the ramp and they looked out to see one of the security guards patrolling the concrete floor.

"Dammit! I knowed them graffiti boys would bring on the security men. We're gonna have an awful time getting' in and outter here."

"I hope yer ain't too hungry right now," Ernest added as he heard Sam's stomach rumble, "'cause we're prob'ly stuck here fer a while. I sure wish we'd have made the Grocery Stop last night. That damned Red Dawg took me astray again." Ernest didn't have to mention the Red Dawg to see that Sam felt the same way. Again, the booze had complicated their lives and made them both uncomfortable. Ernest could see that Sam was hungry and was not pleased with the predicament.

"Don't yer worry none. I'm sure we'll be able to find us a way ter get out at a good time. Just yer hold tight, I'll get 'er figgered out."

The pair waited and watched and listened throughout the day, waiting for a good time to make a run for the door without attracting attention. Several times, they thought the security guard had gone on his way. They quietly made their way out and behind the first row of cars, but each time the guard had come back along his path and they had to return beneath the ramp.

"They're takin' that graffiti pretty serious, ain't they? I guess we'll just have ter wait 'til after the rush hour," Ernest suggested, "Ah'm sure that old guard will have ter take a break then."

Rush hour came and went, and while the original guard was certainly gone, he was simply replaced with a different guard, who dutifully walked a circuit through the garage, never disappearing long enough for Sam and Ernest to make their way up to street level.

"I knows yer hungry and wants ter get outter here, but yer knows we cain't give our positions away if we want ter stay here during some of these cold months. Let's hold out a bit longer. Mah stomach's a growlin' fer sompn' solid, but she'll have ter wait. I'm lucky I at least have a nip o' Red Dawg."

While Ernest settled back in against the wall to have a few more drinks, Sam didn't share his enthusiasm for the booze. Sam's stomach was aching, and he wondered how long he would be willing to trade a warm and private dwelling for the pangs of his hunger.

"I guess we'll have ter wait 'til the mornin' rush to see if we kin sneak outter here," Ernest commented as he took another sip of booze.

Sam worried that he wouldn't make it through the night. He started sifting his way through the dusty trash and wrappers at the low end of the ramp, hoping for a few potato chips or crusts of bread that had gone unnoticed by previous human inhabitants or scavenging rodents, but was disappointed in each corner. Sam slept restlessly, keeping one eye and one ear open for Ernest to start a drunken rant and give their location away to the ever-present security guard. Fortunately, Ernest passed out before the rant could begin.

They woke to the now-familiar sound of car tires squealing down the ramp. Days earlier, Sam had concluded that the tires didn't squeal because of fast or reckless driving, but because of the way the tires slipped along the smooth surface of the concrete floor. Further, the echo of the garage seemed to amplify the effect. Optimistically, Sam looked outside and around the edge of the ramp, hoping to see only commuters, but he was quickly forced back below at the sight of the security guard continuing his rounds. He wondered if he would ever get to eat again, and thought long and hard about giving up their home for a bite of food.

Commuters continued their normal routine, and Sam kept his mind busy listening to the click and clomps of the heels and loafers above.

Ernest finally stirred to life, grumbling, "Damn, ah'm a hungry sumbudabitch. Ah'm a thinkin' I could cook yer up and eat yer."

But Ernest's smile was met with a disapproving stare of hunger from Sam, and Ernest knew that he had given up their safety and comfort for his Red Dawg. Sam could tell that Ernest felt bad, but he wasn't in the mood to be forgiving now.

Putting the rumbling of his stomach out of his mind, Sam listened to a particularly loud set of shoes walking quickly across the concrete. They weren't so loud as a pair of small heels, but were noisy enough, especially as they approached the ramp. Sam worried that they were the shoes of the security guard, as they tapped nearer and nearer with a purposeful pace. While the sound of shoes was common, they rarely came this close to the ramp. He froze as he sensed them to be directly above, and then saw a brown paper grocery sack fall over the edge and land in a heap near the entrance to their shelter.

"Shh!" cautioned Ernest, "Somebody dropped sompn' and they'll sure be down for it shortly. Just be quiet and still, and mebbe they won't notice us."

The pair inched away from the entrance, toward the lower part of the ramp, always keeping their eye toward the crumpled brown paper sack that had just fallen from above. They listened for the sound of those same shoes. They stared motionless waiting and waiting. The shoes of other commuters came and went. Some with hard clacking heels and others with more of a shuffle, but the shoes of the person who dropped the bag did not come back.

They waited until well after the rush hour was finished, and finally started to relax. Sam was almost happy to have this stressful diversion. At least it kept his mind away from his hunger.

"Yer know, I don't think summun's comin' back fer that ol' bag. I wonder if they don't know that they dropped it there. I think we should chance it, and grab that ol' bag to see what's in 'er."

Sam was dubious.

"Yer think summun's gonna trick us with that ol' bag, don'cher?" Ernest whispered, "Well yer may be right, but if they're tryin' ter trap us, they already knows that we're here. So, we may as well jest get 'er done."

Ernest's reasoning was sound, so they crept toward the sack near the entrance. Sam poked his head out and looked around and above the ramp, fully expecting to be met with a blow from the guard's billy-club, but there was no one around. He heard the guard's shoes at a distance, but couldn't see him. Sam grabbed the sack by the top, and quietly dragged it back under the concrete ramp.

"Well looky here!" Ernest smiled as he opened the sack, "Summon's done dropped their groceries right here. I don't think ah've seen anything look better in a long time!"

Ernest set the contents of the sack on the floor as he took inventory. The bounty included a bottle of orange juice, a loaf of bread, a twenty-four-slice package of American cheese singles, three bananas, a Twinkie and a small package of sliced bologna.

"I cain't believe our luck here. I thought we was gonna have ter give up our shelter here to get sompn' ter eat with that old guard keeping' watch," Ernest said, smiling. "This'll hold us over fer a few days at least!"

Ernest set out a few pieces of bread, some cheese and bologna slices, and peeled one of the bananas, and the two wolfed down the ration. Sam had no interest in the banana, which suited Ernest fine. He ceded an extra slice of bologna to Sam in trade.

Ernest seemed to love the orange juice. Sam, although horribly thirsty, had to work to choke down the liquid. He drank because his thirst directed him too, but he vowed to never touch the acidy orange drink again, barring another emergency.

"I really wonder who would drop their groceries like that and not notice?" Ernest pondered, not expecting an answer. "Or, mebbe they knowed they dropped them, but they were too busy or afraid to come down and pick 'em up. I don't know why this sack showed up, but ah'm damned glad it did!"

Sam agreed.

The few days following the appearance of the grocery sack smelled of paint as the last of the graffiti was covered in white, matching the rest of the painted concrete in the garage. Sam found it interesting that the painters went to the trouble of re-painting the areas of the stairwell that hadn't been covered in the graffiti as well. It seemed like a lot of work for the same color.

Ernest had noticed the same, commenting, "Lookit how that new paint is so shiny, even once it's had a chance ter dry. I'll bet that there's some special paint that them graffiti kids will find their spray paint jist won't stick ter. Ah'm hoping them guards will find another place ter be once that new paint's finished up, so we can get out and go fer a stroll. Ah'm startin' to get some cabin fever under this here ramp."

Sam felt the same. The food was a great holdover, and the ramp was a nice shelter from the weather and the cold, but he needed a change of scenery.

Fortunately, the next day, the familiar sound of the guard's shoes was noticeably absent. After the morning rush, Sam and Ernest warily sneaked up and out through the stairwell to get their first glimpse of the outside in more than a week. The sun, while masked behind a thin blanket of grey clouds, was a welcome sight.

11. Christmas

Ernest smiled as he took a deep breath of the cold air. "We still have some dinero from our 'handlin' last week, but ah'm damned dry on mah Red Dawg. Let's take a walk down to the Liquor Mart to get fixed up there."

Sam, while happy to be out from under the ramp, was not pleased with Ernest's immediate dash for the Red Dawg.

"I knows what yer thinking' there Sam. I'll jist spend a little on mah hooch, and we'll head for the Grocery Stop a little later. We can stock up a bit and head back after the evening rush. I ain't in no hurry to get back under there, even if it is pretty cold. Ah'm sure that old yeller coat of yours is keeping' yer plenty warm."

Sam could tolerate this plan, but would still have preferred that Ernest stayed away from the bottle.

The walk down Boulder Avenue to the Liquor Mart was uneventful. The cold was keeping the *rough sleepers*, at least those who hadn't been trapped inside for the last week, in charity shelters and in makeshift homes like Sam and Ernest's parking garage spot. The few commuters and business people on the streets were abrupt and purposeful as they traversed the sidewalks, working to go from warm car to warm building as quickly as possible.

The sun was near it's high point for the day when Sam and Ernest arrived at the Liquor Mart, although at this time of year the zenith was set far in the south and it didn't provide much additional warmth. Sam waited outside while Ernest made his purchase. He was the only customer in the store, so he had no opportunity to pilfer an extra bottle. The disappointment was clear on Ernest's face as he exited.

"I guess I'll have ter do with only one bottle fer now," he lamented, as he flashed his one bottle neatly wrapped in a brown paper bag. "Let's head down ter the river to see if anything's happenin' down there before we head back for the Grocery Stop."

Sam wasn't hungry yet, so he didn't complain. The pair wandered through the historic neighborhood between downtown and the river, taking care not to attract any more attention than they had to. Ernest, who had been rationing his Red Dawg during the forced stay under the parking ramp, nipped at the bottle continuously during the walk. By the time they made it to the trail along the river, Ernest was unable to walk a straight line and was slurring his speech more than usual. The trail was deserted, aside from a few hearty mountain bikers out to get some exercise on a cold winter's day.

"Sam, ah'm gonna have ter sit mahself down on that thar bench fer a bit and catch mah breath," he sputtered, as he half-sat and half-fell onto the first bench they encountered.

Sam knew that it would be more than a "bit," as Ernest laid down across the length of the bench and quickly began snoring. Sam debated on whether to go off exploring on his own while Ernest destroyed himself, but decided to stay put when Ernest began one of his sleeping rants.

He wailed in his typical drunken tone, "I knows I kin take care o' you and them kids now, Shondra Lee! I'll go find me a job and I'll take good care o'you. I miss yer so much, honey. Kin I puhleeze come home?"

Sam nudged Ernest to quiet him, lest someone call the authorities. He could feel Ernest's pain, and knew that if Ernest stayed away from the bottle, he could take care of himself. Yet, he was always drawn back to the Red Dawg.

When it was clear that Ernest was going to take an extended doze, Sam decided to stretch his legs and wander around a bit. The walk from the garage to the Liquor Mart to the river had felt wonderful after having been cooped up for a week, and so why not keep that going? He traveled south on the trail, following the river, trotting, almost jogging, and realizing how much slower he moved when he was with Ernest. Sam eventually found the familiar metal park bench marking the turn off the trail to the tent village where he and Ernest had stayed many weeks ago.

"Why not visit?" he thought, and so he turned off the trail and made his way through the brush to find the clearing. The tents were still there, shabby, but functional. There was no activity outside, so he poked his nose into Rosine's tent hoping to find a friendly face.

"Well, hi there, honey!" Rosine gushed, "What are you up to, Sam? It's great to see you. It doesn't look like you brought Ernest with you. I hope he's okay."

Sam smiled back, but as he did, Gerald came into the tent from behind him.

"What are you doing here, you sum' bitch? I hope you had enough sense to ditch that old Ernest feller. He's nothing but trouble! He damned sure better not have come back here." Gerald was as blunt as usual.

"Give him a break, Gerald. Ernest didn't come along, so you can get off your high horse there."

"It's good to see you, Sam," Edwin followed Gerald with a little more grace. "We're doing okay for food, but we certainly miss the rabbits you used to find. You look well-fed, so I assume life is treating you well."

"Did you lose Ernest?" Rosine persisted. "If you did, maybe you should come join us again!"

"No, Rosine, that's just another mouth to feed," Gerald piped in without hesitation.

Rosine looked at Edwin for an argument, but he had none, "Rosine, you must understand that we'll have to make some changes soon. With the power company having found us out and stopped us from tapping into the light post, they will certainly point the authorities at us. Even if they don't find us, we will certainly have to move before it gets very cold. If we don't, we'll freeze in the winter air."

Rosine understood. "I'm sorry, honey," she lamented, "but maybe we can talk more once we get re-settled. You're welcome to hang around for a while though, if you want."

Gerald cleared his throat in disapproval.

Sam was perplexed at the conversation anyway. He was paying a friendly visit, and all three of these people were debating whether he could live with them. Sam smiled, paid his respects to all, and went on his way back toward Ernest. He knew that he would not want to abandon Ernest. While his liquor habit was annoying and sometimes uncomfortable, he and Ernest were a good team. Sam didn't see any reason to break that up. The tent village was an interesting opportunity, but it wasn't all that comfortable, and it seemed that Edwin, Gerald and Rosine were in for some trying times as the weather turned colder.

Sam wandered aimlessly around the river trail, seeing only a few runners and walkers out in the cold. He found garland and white lights decorating the pedestrian bridge, and saw that all the light poles had been transformed into "candy canes" with striped ribbons since he had last walked this path. The children's splash pad, near the 41st Street park, was completely abandoned, but there were several children bouncing around the nearby playground. Sam could see the mothers of the children eyeing him carefully, worried he was a threat to their brood. Sam had no interest in the children beyond simple amusement and curiosity. He knew that Ernest dearly missed his children. And, based on Ernest's encounter on the trail months ago, he knew that the children here at the playground were about the same age as Ernest's. He wondered what it was that called to Ernest as he embraced his Red Dawg. He wondered how that could be more important than the children he loved. He wondered whether Ernest would find a way back to these people he missed so much. If he ever did, Sam wondered how he would fare without his friend. Aside from his own self interest, Sam knew that Ernest's family was the only thing holding him back from complete self-destruction. He wanted to do something for him, but knew that any argument against the Red Dawg would only push Ernest farther down the slope. He found it perplexing that he was unable to help his friend.

Sam eventually made his way back up the trail, and found his friend in the same position on the same bench as when he left him. His mouth was slightly open and saliva was drooling across his cheek. His nose had brightened significantly from when he left, likely a combination of the cool weather and the alcohol binge. Sam gave him a friendly nudge.

"I love yer, I do, Shondra Lee! I jist wants to take care of them kids an' yer. I hope yer'll..." Ernest sputtered before he sunk back to his restless sleep.

Sam gave him another push, firmer and less friendly, rolling him from the bench into a lump on the sidewalk below the bench. He wouldn't have ordinarily been so rough, but Sam was frustrated by Ernest's behavior and was starting to get a little hungry too.

"Dammit! I must've rolled of'n that old bench. This here concrete is pretty solid. It shore as hell woke this ol' man up!"

Sam's nudge was successful;Ernest was clearly jolted free from his drunken slumber.

"Well, Sam, it looks like I had me a little siesta. Ah'm glad yer close by, cuz ah'm feelin' a little hollow on the inside. I feel like I could eat the rest of the night. Let's go make a run ter the Grocery Stop before it gets too dark, and we'll spend a little of our handlin' dough on some chow."

While Sam was still a little perturbed at Ernest, the idea of dinner settled him down, and the pair marched their way back up the steep hill on Denver Avenue to the Grocery Stop. Per their usual process, Sam waited outside while Ernest practiced his patented "five finger discount" shopping. He politely paid for a loaf of bread, some grape jelly and a bag of plain potato chips. Of course, he also walked out with a package of American cheese slices, bologna and some hotdogs hidden in his jacket, to round out the meal. Once they were a safe distance away, Ernest moved the meat and cheese into the grocery bag, and they proceeded back toward downtown and their garage.

By now, night had fallen and the city was lit only by automobile and street lights. Rush hour had come and gone, yet the streets were a bit busier than usual for a Friday night. They noticed several cars with pine trees tied to their roofs with twine, the loose needles littering the streets as they drove past.

"Looks like it's time fer Christmas, there Sam. I loves Christmas. It's the time when Our Savior, Jesus, was born. Heaven knows that ol' bastards like us needs us some Jesus. We sure cain't afford one of them trees, though. But ah'd sure like ter have one. It would remind me of mah fam'ly. I think I jist might read some 'o my Bible tonight," Ernest declared. "Hell, we couldn't fit no decent tree under our ramp even if we could sneak 'er by them guards."

The moon was rising in the east as they crossed over Sixth Street and turned toward the garage. They found that, with the rush hour traffic having subsided, crews were busy blocking the inner streets from automobile traffic, allowing only pedestrians through on most streets.

"Look at them metal barriers that the police is puttin' up. I'll bet'cher that ol' parade o' lights is gonna happen ternight. I loves me a Christmas parade! It's one of them things that brings out a load 'o people ter downtown - even more than Church on Sundays! If we can get this here food back under our ramp, the cold'll keep it fresh and we can prob'ly panhandle up a storm! There'll be a load of parents with their littlen's that would rather hand us a dollar than have a quick conversation, so we'll make out like bandits!

We'll be set fer chow and Red Dawg fer the next week! We're in luck, fer damned sure! I loves me some Christmas!"

The crowds hadn't started to fill downtown yet, so Sam and Ernest's parking garage was empty with the exception of a few straggling cars from commuters who were working late. The pair silently crept down the freshly painted stairwell and along the garage wall, eventually darting under the ramp.

Ernest tore open the bologna and cheese and tossed several slices of each to Sam.

"Eat up, right quick, and let's go git us some more dinero!" Ernest smiled between bites of bologna and cheese. "We're gonna do great ternight! We needs ter get outter here and find a good spot by the beginning' of the parade route ter do the best. Stuff that chow down, and let's go!"

Stomachs full, they traced their steps back across the garage and up the stairwell, then, made their way a few blocks north, near the beginning of the parade route.

"If we're near the start, we can foller ol' Saint Nick up the route. He's the last one in the parade, so everyone stays ter see 'im, but they all head out as soon as he passes. We kin jis foller him along and ask fer donations as folks leaves the parade. What kind of rich suburban daddy is gonna turn down a man in need during the Christmas season, right in front of his fam'ly and right after ol' Saint Nick jist passed him by? We jist might be in food and booze fer weeks!"

They found their way to an massive parking lot by the community college, which was now serving as a staging area for the parade participants. Sam was awestruck by the activity.

There were cowboys and cowgirls brushing and cleaning their horses, many of whom were outfitted in shiny garland. The horses snorted and watched warily as Sam and Ernest walked by, but the animals didn't move or panic. To Sam, the creatures were immense, and he found it ironic that an animal with that size and power would willingly allow a human to ride it and order it around. The smell around the horses was strong, almost like that of the alleys around downtown, but the handlers were vigilant about cleaning up after their animals.

The parade floats were full of light and very noisy. Some were simply pickup trucks decorated for the event, with flatbed trailers to carry a nativity scene and singing children. Others were completely transformed automobiles that appeared to have no function other than to perform as a parade float. They took the shapes of stables and sleighs and snowmen.

Clowns wandered among the floats and cowboys, clumping in groups here and there. High school students gathered with their musical instruments, forming straight lines and playing scales to prepare for their marching band performances. The drums in the bands were particularly loud, so Sam moved quickly around them.

Of all the participants, the marching bands looked to be the most uncomfortable. Sam didn't know if the shiny uniforms they wore didn't provide much warmth in the weather, or if the kids were simply nervous at the prospect of performing in front of thousands of people. He was surprised that the horses, who he thought would be the most tense, appeared to be completely at ease with all the noise and activity surrounding them.

They wandered back and forth through the rows of floats and bands and clowns, taking in the excitement and looking for the best place to follow Santa Claus. Most of the participants ignored the pair. Either they were too busy to take note, or chose to avoid eye contact for fear of starting an unwelcome conversation. No matter the reason, Sam thought it odd that he felt so alone in such a huge crowd of activity.

"There's ole Saint Nick!" Ernest smiled and pointed, "Let's stay over yonder there beyond Santa, and we'll just casually foller him as he heads out. If we stay too close, them police will run us off fer sure, so we'd best just stay some yards behind him. We'll lose a customer or two that way, but it's better'n gittin' evicted by the law."

Sam followed Ernest a few yards behind the Santa Claus float to sit on a curb surrounding a grassy median in the parking lot. The thinning Bermuda grass was dry and rough, having gone dormant weeks earlier from the cooling temperatures. Nonetheless, it was much softer than the concrete bed that Sam had become accustomed to, so he took the opportunity to stretch out and relax. He closed one eye, but kept the other watchful on the activity around him. He could see the parade marshals pointing and waving to the different floats as they brought them up to the starting area for their proper position in line. They would point to a float, then a marching band, then a few more floats and some horses, then a few more floats and another marching band. Then, the cycle would continue. Given the noise that the bands would produce as they marched out onto the parade route, Sam thought it was clever that the organizers separated them with tamer participants.

One by one, the parade convoy cleared the parking lot, making it less and less crowded and quieter by the minute.

Finally, only Santa remained and the marshals began waving him into place on the parade route. Sam and Ernest rose warily, looking around to see a handful of other *rough sleepers* with intentions similar to theirs. Three motorcycle policemen, dressed in warm, thick riding gear rode behind Santa as an escort. Sam could see that the policemen were very aware of their presence and he expected that would certainly intervene if a *rough sleeper* came too close. As a result, they kept their distance, as did the other panhandlers.

As Santa entered the parade, Sam could hear the clapping of hands and squeals of small children, along with the repetitive "Merry Christmas!" that Santa began bellowing as soon as he was illuminated by the street lights of the parade route. Once his float was completely on the street, the parade marshals moved metal barriers behind him to keep the crew of panhandlers and other onlookers from following the parade into the street. As a result, Sam and Ernest were forced into the waving crowd of onlookers. Sam worried about the effect, but soon found that it was a better situation for them to be in and among all the people.

Ernest was already working the crowd. For every "Merry Christmas" that Santa spouted, Ernest would make eye contact with a "customer" and plead, "Could yer share some of that Christmas spirit with a poor soul who's down on his luck? I could sure use some warmth and food if yer could just spare a bit 'o change!" He held out his hat with a few coins and a couple of bills in it to prime the pump, and he had very few declines. Sam could see that Ernest was truly in his element. He was a master in this environment. Each time Ernest's hat would look heavy with change in the least bit, he would deftly transfer the coins and paper to his jacket pocket and keep the flow going. Surely, with this bounty, they would not be hungry for a month. Sam was elated – Christmas was, indeed, a great time of year.

The parade route wove through downtown for at least a mile, and by the time the pair had followed Santa's float all the way through it, the area was starting to quiet down again. There were far fewer customers at the end than at the beginning, but they were consistently willing to give to the cause. Ernest's pockets were noticeably weighed down by the change. It was not something the average customer would notice, but it was evident to Sam.

The parade ended where it started, and the pair made their way back into the large parking lot. Floats, clowns and bands were still there, repacking their equipment and animals for the trip back to wherever they came from. Sam and Ernest found their way to the same grassy median they had visited before, and sat down to collect themselves.

Ernest wore a massive grin, exclaiming, "Sam, I think we're in better shape than we've been in fer a long while. I cain't count all this right now, but I knows it'll add up ter a nice sum. We'll be able to stay clean with our necessities fer a long time. I loves me some Christmas parade!" Sam smiled back at him. "Let's us just stay here fer a bit, let this mess clear out, and we'll head fer our ramp ter finish up our dinner."

Sam was happy with that plan. He watched some of the other panhandlers finishing their way through the parade route. Their smiles told a story similar to Ernest's.

The parking lot was bustling for at least another twenty minutes as the bands loaded onto school buses and the horses loaded onto trailers. Sam saw Santa take his hat and coat off as he sat down in his Subaru, and he watched the clowns remove their colored hair and strange shoes before getting into their cars and motoring away.

As the parking lot cleared, Ernest rose and motioned to Sam saying, "I thinks it's clear enough fer us ter head out, are yer ready ter go?"

Sam nodded and rose as well, and the pair set off in route to their ramp.

While the staging parking lot had certainly emptied out, Sam was surprised at the amount of traffic still on the street. Cars full of families were slowly making their way out of downtown, and many of the streets had been closed for the parade. As a result, the traffic had been backing up since the parade had finished. Drivers had quickly lost the Christmas spirit, and were honking and waving at others who didn't make their way through the intersections fast enough. There was a bottleneck near Sam and Ernest's parking garage that snaked at least three traffic lights back packed with impatient drivers honking and yelling to get through.

"Well, I guess we're lucky that they're all clearin' out of our garage. That ought ter be enough activity fer them guards that they won't notice us." Ernest found the silver lining in yet another grey cloud.

The pair watched the traffic before finding a break to cross the five-lane street. Sam trotted across, while Ernest maintained his usual slow shuffle. As Sam turned around to watch and wait, the horror of the scene moved slowly in front of him. He was helpless, unable to change the events he witnessed.

Ernest's slow gait had him approaching the middle of the street when the traffic light changed to green. A light grey minivan, piloted by a middle-aged woman, was in the in the center lane where Ernest was still shuffling along, and the driver slowed to let him cross. Ernest was appreciative, and gave the minivan driver a friendly wave as he continued across the lane. Yet, as he waved, a small sedan was butted up behind the minivan, inches away from the van's rear bumper. Sam could hear the small car's engine racing and he could see the driver drumming his fingers across the steering wheel with impatience. When he wasn't drumming his fingers, he was twisting the hairs of his long mustache between his fingers. Sam could hear the anger in the driver's voice, though what he was saying wasn't clear. The driver was obviously ready to be on his way, taking his family home after a cold evening at the parade. The sedan was close enough to the van that the mustached man could not see around it. Yet, when he noticed the traffic in the adjoining lane resting back at the light, he jumped at the opportunity to change lanes and zip ahead. The driver pulled the small sedan smartly around the stopped minivan, and glared spitefully up at the driver of the van as he passed. He looked to the front just in time to see a raggedy vagabond shuffling across his lane. There was no time for him to move his foot from the gas to the brake. Ernest flew upward from the impact of the sedan's bumper, rolling across the windshield, cracking it near the middle so it looked like a spider's web.

Sam saw Ernest come to a rest, momentarily, on top of the car. His eyes were wild with fear, and the coins from his pockets were being thrown across the top of the car and around the street. Sam could hear the jingling of the coins hitting the pavement like rain, then the squealing of skidding tires covered the sound of the coins. The driver had panicked and slammed on his brakes, causing Ernest to abruptly roll off the front of the car. Ernest's head hit the asphalt and bounced, and at that moment, Sam saw the fear vanish from Ernest's eyes. Ernest's momentum carried him further down the street as the car skidded to a stop before him. His arms and legs flailed helplessly as he rolled, and lay in unnatural positions when he came to a rest.

Sam surveyed the scene from his perch on the curb. All the traffic on the one-way street was now stopped. The driver of the minivan was shaking and sobbing behind the wheel. The mustached driver had jumped out of his car, running toward Ernest, while his family stared silently from the car. The driver's face had taken on the same fear that Sam had seen on Ernest's face only moments before while in the midst of his fall. Other drivers and pedestrians began to run toward Ernest, most shaking their heads, wide-eyed with shock.

While he was afraid of the mass of people beginning to form, Sam wanted to help his friend. He weaved his way through the onlookers, seeing the pennies and dimes from Ernest's pockets littering the pavement. Thankfully, Ernest's eyes were open and moving, though blood covered his head and face.

Ernest took note of Sam and called out, "Sam! Yer come over here right quick."

Sam was reluctant to push through the crowd much more, but complied at the request of his friend.

"I guess I really messed that one up. There'll be an am-bu-lance here ter scrape me up soon, I reckon. I'll bet they'll take mah away fer sure, cuz I ain't doin' no walkin like this." He nodded to the twisted legs attached to his body. "Yer take care of yerself, ya hear? If this here crash don't send me home fer good and if I kin git loose o' them

---

authorities, I'll find yer again. I'll look fer yer in our usual spots, so just yer be common. Don't worry about me none, though. Yer knows that I kin take care o' mahself. Hell, I kin even help take care o' yer. If this ain't happened, who knows, mebbe I could have gone home to mah Shondra Lee and took care o' her and them children. I'll prob'ly never know now. Ah'm so sorry fer leavin' yer behind!" Ernest grimaced in obvious pain. "Now, yer head on out. I kin hear them sirens, so there's gonna be am-bu-lance and po-lice all around in nothin' flat. I'll miss yer, brother! Now, git!"

While Sam didn't want to leave his friend, he knew there was nothing he could do to help. He also understood that, if the police or other authorities were to find him here, he might be taken away as well. Sam knew that the best thing to do was to leave. He nodded to his friend - his best friend - then turned and sauntered across the street to the sidewalk to take his place with the rest of the crowd. He watched the paramedics as they tended to Ernest's immediate needs, then carefully placed him on a stretcher and moved him toward the waiting ambulance. Ernest's arms and legs were still in unusual positions. His eyes were open and moving, and the ambulance attendants did not cover his face. Sam was comforted, somewhat, at being able to see the life in his friend when the ambulance doors closed.

The crowd around Sam was largely sympathetic to Ernest's pain and the scary scene around them. However, they could easily see Ernest's vagabond lifestyle choice in the clothes that he wore and the coins in his pockets, which somehow made them feel better about it. "This guy won't be paying his ambulance bill – that I can promise you," were the words from one of the onlookers.

Sam didn't argue. He just watched the ambulance speed away, wondering what would come next.

12. Solo

Somehow, automatically, Sam found his way back below the ramp in the parking garage. When he arrived, he had no idea if he had been seen or followed. He didn't remember if he had been stealthy crossing the garage. He could have walked right by one of the guards, smiled at him and then ducked under the ramp right in front of the guard for all he knew. He didn't remember any part of how he traveled from when he left Ernest to when he arrived at the ramp. He just knew that the space beneath the ramp was home. At least for now.

Sam felt lost. He felt much like he did before he and Ernest had met. In those days, he had wandered about the streets without any destination in mind. He had ambled aimlessly in search of his next meal or his next shelter. He had never put any thought into what he needed for any moment other than the present. When he was hungry, he dug through Dumpsters or ferreted through spent lunch bags left along the sidewalks. When he was thirsty, he found his way to a fountain or puddle. When he was cold, he would find an alley that sheltered him from the wind and cover himself with newspaper or cardboard or whatever was convenient. There was no forethought, there was no plan, there was no destination. Did he want to return to that life? It really wasn't so much *life* as it was *existence*. In that time, he had no friends and he had no purpose. His time was without form or function. It simply was.

He was too tired and lost to consider such deep thoughts. He felt the pain of losing his friend, along with the anxiety associated with the uncertainty that was his future. He took a few deep breaths, taking care to feel the cool air filling his lungs. He watched the steam blow from his nostrils as he exhaled the air, warmed by his body, back into the chilly air of the parking garage. He was happy to be alive, and he wanted to appreciate it. Yet, so much of his life was now gone.

Sam slowly ate the few pieces of cheese that remained under the ramp, and then fell into a hard but fitful sleep. He remembered and dreamed of his times both before and with Ernest. Remembering was not something that came easy to Sam, and he wondered why the memories were flowing through his brain so frequently this night. He dreamed of his times with Ernest, remembering the cons at the churches, the panhandling, the food runs in the Grocery Stop and chasing the rabbits. He remembered Ernest gathering up liquor from near-empty bottles, forming his own medicine to melt him into a stupor. He remembered living in the culvert by the river, and the squeak of the shopping cart wheels. He remembered Ernest passing out from his drinking.

Sam thought it was novel to remember – it wasn't something he had done much of before he met Ernest.

Sam slept, and dreamed, and slept. He would wake when he was no longer tired or when he was hungry or thirsty. He snacked on the remaining food below the ramp when he was hungry. The light rain coming down over those days dribbled across the concrete near the ramp, so he drank from that stream whenever he felt thirsty.

If he had felt confined earlier when the guard had him trapped below the ramp, he was quite content at this point to simply stay put. The surroundings in his concrete hovel beneath the ramp really hadn't changed - only Sam's attitude toward staying in there. He had no desire to go out and forage, yet he eventually ran out of food. But even then, he stayed quietly under the ramp, sleeping and dreaming. It wasn't until the emptiness in his stomach was unbearable and he was beginning to feel weak that Sam decided that he should go back out into the world.

That day, like many in the heart of the Oklahoma winter, was blustery and grey. If he looked closely up at the clouds, he could see them moving rapidly in the wind. However, the grey cover was consistent, so at a glance it just appeared as a stationary blanket. It was cold, but not harshly so. The wind found its way around the downtown buildings and cut through Sam's coat as if to make sure he remembered that *winter* was in charge.

Sam ambled up the sidewalk on Boston Avenue this lonely Thursday morning, ducking into shop doors when the wind gusted heavily. He noticed all the business people around him, and felt they were watching him more closely than he would have preferred. These people, who before had appeared to be uninterested in Sam and Ernest, now appeared to be watching his movements closely. It seemed they were sizing him up, working to determine whether he was predator or prey. Sam observed that each person was eyeing him cautiously and carefully. He had certainly not noticed that feeling when he and Ernest had walked the streets together. What was different now, Sam wondered? Why did these people suddenly take a closer interest in him? Did they expect that *rough sleepers* stayed in pairs? Did Sam look particularly rough after his time beneath the ramp? Sam found his reflection in a window glass, and saw nothing unexpected. He was not particularly clean, but his eyes and face and coat all appeared to be as he expected. He shrugged the extra attention off, assuming that when he was with Ernest he simply hadn't noticed.

Sam made his way to the fountain in Bartlett Square, since he was more thirsty than hungry. The fountain wasn't operating, but there was water in the bottom, so Sam found the cleanest place to have a quick drink. He noticed the nickels and pennies laying on the bottom, tossed in by children making a wish or lovers making a promise, and thought that Ernest would have been proud to scoop them up to apply to his Red Dawg fund. That wasn't Sam's style, however, so he admired the shiny ones as he drank and then left the coins where they were.

Thirst satisfied, he paid a quick trip to the alley behind the best of the uptown hotels. He wasn't patient enough to wait for a warm bag of scraps, so he hopped into the Dumpster and found a black garbage bag near the top of the heap that, from the look of the shapes and bulges, held the promise of roasted chicken. Tearing the bag open with his teeth, he was disappointed to find the shapes had been deceiving. They were just plastic plates and cups. However, remnants of scrambled eggs and bacon were sandwiched between and provided a tasty breakfast. Sam pulled top plates from the pile, cleaned off the bacon and egg scraps and then moved on to the next. He skipped the ones where the spilled plastic cups had soaked the eggs in cold coffee or orange juice, but the ones with milk tasted quite good to him.

As he was finishing his meal, Sam heard a door open and footsteps move toward the Dumpster. Taking that cue, Sam hopped back into the alley, fully startling the busboy bringing out a fresh bag of garbage.

"Get out of here, you dirty bastard!" The busboy was clearly surprised at Sam's leap from the trash bin. "You make a mess of the alley, and then I have to clean it up!"

Sam wasn't particularly interested in the rant. He looked back at the busboy and smiled as he trotted down the alley toward Boston Avenue. Curiously, the busboy smiled back. Sam was intrigued by the smile, but then saw the glass jelly jar in the busboy's hand and realized that the smile was not a friendly one. He accelerated from a trot to a run, but the busboy had a good arm, and Sam saw a flash of liquid as the small jar shattered on the back of his head. Some of the liquid was his blood and some was strawberry jelly. Sam yelped with surprise, but continued running out of the alley.

"Remember that the next time you go digging through my trash!" the busboy called, adding, "Next time I'll have something bigger for you!" The busboy was still smiling, his fist defiantly in the air.

Sam's head hurt, but not enough to slow him down. He scurried back to the garage, and boldly walked through to take his place under the ramp. He wasn't sure why, but at this point he didn't really care if the security officers saw him enter or came to chase him out. As best he could, he used Ernest's old blankets to remove the blood and jelly from the hair on the back of his head. Once clean, he decided that he should leave the ramp to find a new home and some new friends. It was a risk, Sam knew, because of the cold weather and the temperament of the *rough sleepers*, but he knew he had to find some companionship again. After spending so much time with Ernest as a close friend, Sam knew that a human relationship was a key ingredient in his life.

His first thought came back to Rosine. She, and even Gerald and Edwin, had been kind to him during his last visit, especially considering his relationship with Ernest and the problems that his friend had presented. While there was a possibility that they still may not want Sam to live with them, he felt it was worth a trip to the river to find out.

Again, without regard to being seen by the security guards, Sam made his way out of the garage and sauntered south toward the river. As he walked, he wondered about the clearing and the tents, and especially about whether Gerald would accept him. After the days of isolation, the uncomfortable stares of the people around him, and the disposition of the busboy with his glass jelly jar, Sam was looking forward to some kind words from Rosine. Surely she would accept him and make him feel welcome. He wouldn't ask for food, so Gerald and Edwin would not be put out. He really just needed a friend.

Sam walked faster and faster in anticipation, until he found himself at a light trot going down Denver Avenue. He was so immersed in his anticipation of some friendly human contact that he didn't even notice the rain falling from the blanket of clouds. He didn't notice the group of *rough sleepers* using the bus stop in front of the Grocery Stop for a shelter. He didn't bother to look for traffic on Riverside Drive as he crossed the busy boulevard until he heard the slipping of tires and the blare of a horn as a sedan slid toward him on the street. Startled, Sam jumped straight up and watched the hood of the car pass underneath him. His body landed solidly on the windshield, creating a spider web of broken glass directly in front of the driver. The car slid to a halt with Sam still on top, and Sam sat up on the hood to collect himself. He fully expected that his fate would be like Ernest's – an inability to move, a crowd gathering around, pain and moaning. While he was knocked breathless, he was quickly able to fill his lungs again. He felt his limbs and searched his body for pain. The biggest offender was still the back of his head where the jelly jar had landed. Sam looked through the cracked windshield at the driver, a woman whose fingers were so tightly wound around the steering wheel that her knuckles had turned completely white. She stared up at Sam, but didn't move. Other cars had stopped, but none of the drivers were interested in getting out into the rain, so the traffic had simply stopped.

Sam considered rolling down onto the pavement and waiting for the ambulance. After all, that's what Ernest had done. However, Sam took another inventory of his limbs and found that he really didn't hurt that badly. So, he simply went back to his original plan – finding Rosine! He slid off the hood of the car, turned to nod at the flustered driver, and then restarted his jog through the cold rain. He forced a smile through the bruises as he left the snarl of traffic on Riverside Drive behind him and made his way onto the river trail.

Since he was already soaked to the bone and because he was still working to catch his breath, Sam slowed to a comfortable walk once he was on the trail. He took time to appreciate the beauty of the rain lightly falling around him, pooling on the trail and running off the foliage lining the river. The scene reminded of him of his last long rainy walk with Ernest. He imagined the squeak of the shopping cart wheels as they walked side-by-side, covered in their garbage-bag ponchos. The memory made Sam smile, yet the idea that he was actually paying attention to his memories didn't really occur to him.

Sam found the wide place in the trail with the park bench, effectively pointing him to the clearing. He stopped briefly to convince himself that it was the right entrance. Once confirmed, his confidence carried him as he darted deftly behind the bench and through the reeds, working to approach the clearing.

The tents were set as Sam expected, still neatly arranged between the scrub brush and the river. They were close enough to the bridge to be difficult to see from an observer above. He didn't expect any activity outside the tents given the dismal weather, and he wasn't surprised to see the clearing quiet. He listened carefully, working to filter out the sound of the rain, but couldn't tell if anyone was inside Rosine's tent. Since knocking was impractical, he poked his nose through the tent flaps to find the dwelling empty. From there, he correctly assumed that the trio would be assembled in Edwin's tall tent and was surprised at the warm welcome he received.

"Why, hello, Sam!" Rosine exclaimed as he politely nosed his way between the front flaps of the large tent. As expected, Edwin was seated near one of his books, straining to read in the dim light. Gerald and Rosine were engaged in a some sort of card game. "It's great to see you, Hon! What are you doing out in this weather?"

Sam didn't have a pat answer for her.

"I'm sorry to hear about Ernest. We heard that he had a hard time with a car the other night. I guess everyone knows who Ernest is, 'cause it's all over the street. I suspect that he'll be put in an institution if he lived. We'll probably never know. Probably better for him to pass, as I know he wouldn't like to be confined. He's a *rough sleeper*, through and through, and I know he wouldn't do well in a domesticated place. Poor Ernest!"

Sam wasn't sure he agreed with Rosine. While Ernest was certainly an expert in navigating the streets, his frequent binges and cries for his wife made Sam think that Ernest might do well off the street if the circumstances were right. That is, if he could make a proper home with his family.

"Well, I'm happy to see ya out on your own without that Ernest bastard," Gerald piped in. "Believe me, you're better off without..."

"Oh, dry up Gerald," Rosine interrupted. "Sam and Ernest were a great pair. Sam, honey, you're welcome to hole up with us for a while. Why don't you go get settled in my tent, and I'll come check in on you in a bit."

Gerald glanced at Edwin, who looked up from his book only long enough to nod at Rosine and roll his eyes at Gerald.

"It's a damned good thing that you can contribute," Gerald conceded. "If that worthless Ernest was still with you, you'd be walking away now!" Gerald stomped out of Edwin's tent in a bit of a huff. Sam was not surprised.

"Don't mind him," Rosine apologized, "Go on. I'll catch up. Sorry it's a bit cold over there. We lost our electric service a while back, so we're really campin' now!"

"It'll be OK," Sam heard Rosine explain to Edwin as he made his way to her tent, "You know he can take care of himself and he can help us too. Gerald will get over it."

That evening, like the first night he and Ernest had slept in the tent village those months ago, Sam wondered if this was a place he could stay for a while. Rosine was always so welcoming, Gerald was hostile, and Edwin was simply indifferent. After his time with Ernest, Sam knew that he needed companionship. The big question was whether the companionship he could find here at the clearing was what he needed.

What Sam did know was that having some friendly people around made him more comfortable. In the wake of losing Ernest, Sam knew he needed all the comfort he could find.

13. Fishing

As the new year began, men in bright vests promptly removed the cheery lights of Christmas from street lamps along the river trail. Only a grey, winter sky replaced the sparkle of the lights. In Sam's opinion, the gloomy clouds were not an adequate substitute.

The short days brought colder temperatures, and without the electricity of the previous winter, the tents became colder and drearier with each night.

Sam and Rosine made several panhandling trips to their favorite corners. While some customers felt compassion for the pair on such cold and cloudy days, most were unwilling to open their windows to the chill and damp of the Oklahoma winter. Rosine brought back as much food as the meager alms would provide, but she was not as good as Ernest with the five-finger discount and so it was rarely enough to satisfy the four inhabitants of the tent village. Occasionally, she would find a candle or a sterno – just enough to provide a little heat in the tent. But, of course, such small items would only last a night or two before they were exhausted.

One afternoon, Sam found it curious that the downtown traffic was building well before dusk, certainly earlier than he would have expected the rush hour. He watched from the edge of the river trail as the cars poured down Houston and Denver avenues. He couldn't believe that the confined downtown area could possibly hold so many cars, even with the multi-level parking garages like he and Ernest had inhabited. Riverside Drive eventually became a solid line of cars, two across with their red tail lights flickering as far south as Sam could see.

He ambled back to the tent village as a light rain began to fall, and ducked into Edwin's tent to be friendly. Both Edwin and Gerald were seated on the floor, both reading by the low light. Gerald nodded at Sam and tossed over a slice of bologna.

"Eat up, son!" he exclaimed, "There ain't much left! We're gonna be hungry tomorrow, cause I know you and Rosine ain't hit it big in better'n a week!"

"You know, Gerald," Edwin looked up from his book, "you and Sam should go on a quick fishing trip before evening sets in. It's not raining hard, and the water is pretty low. You can probably catch a few and we'll have something to eat over the next couple of days."

Gerald wasn't amused. His face turned down as he grumbled, "Dammit, Edwin! You know I don't like the water. Especially when it's cold like this! I'll just do without eating for a few days."

"Possibly you will, but what about Rosine and me?" Edwin smiled, knowing he could coax his friend. "We would both very much appreciate some food."

"Oh, come on Edwin! There ain't no water in the river anyway!" Gerald snorted.

"Ah, but you see, my friend, the river recedes and makes some things more difficult, but it also makes some things easier."

Edwin smiled and jumped into the back of his tent, rustling in a corner for a bit, and finally emerging with a mesh bag about the size of a pillow case. The bag looked to be originally white in color, but had splotches of brown and green all over. Sam could smell the oil from the skin of fish on the bag. It was strangely repulsive, yet also made his mouth water as he thought of eating the fish. Edwin also carried a piece of nylon rope with a skewer on the end and a long, barbed pole.

"If you two can make your way down to the walking bridge, you'll find that the water is very low on the other side of it. In this weather, I doubt that there will be people fishing with poles, but if they are, they will be on the north side. You will want to ignore them and get down to the river's edge on the south side. If you look in the shallow water, I suspect that you'll find some fish that are trapped. Get a few good ones, and try not to bring too much attention to yourselves!"

"I'm not much of a swimmer, ya know," Gerald objected, "And I'm not getting in no running river!"

"Then, I suggest that you use your gift of charm to persuade Sam into doing the corralling, and you do the stabbing and bagging."

Edwin looked at him knowingly over the rims of his glasses and smiled.

Gerald caved.

"Come on, you som' bitch," he called to Sam, staying far away from any charm. "I'll show you how we can catch some dinner. I'm sure there won't be any competition, 'cause there's nobody else crazy enough to be out on the river on an evening like this."

P.D. Bruns

Sam watched as Gerald snatched the net and pole out of Edwin's hands. He didn't exactly feel threatened by the equipment, but it didn't make him comfortable to be around it either. He followed Gerald through the mist, out past the bench and onto the trail.

They followed the trail, running parallel to both the river and to Riverside Drive. They watched the line of red tail lights, moving at a crawl down the boulevard. The pair, the only ones walking on the trail at the time, were moving faster than the cars on the street.

"I'm glad it's so gloomy tonight," Gerald snickered. "If there were families along the trail, they'd be worried about a pair like us walking down the trail with a big spear like this one!" He shook the spear above his head with a smile.

"Of course, I really like carrying it. Edwin would say that it makes me feel primal! We'll have some good fun if we see some fish!"

Sam didn't think he had seen Gerald quite so happy. Ever. It appeared that having this fierce weapon at his command really put Gerald in good spirits.

"I wonder why there's so much traffic so early today," Gerald asked aloud as he watched the traffic on the street, "I don't think it's a holiday.'

They continued down the trail.

"I'll bet there's some weather coming this way – probably some good snow or ice. All these *professionals* are probably hurryin' home to stay out of the wet. We don't have to worry about our commute so much, but we'd better get our fishin' done before it starts in. I'd much rather be in my tent when the sky opens up. It may still be cold, but at least it won't be real wet."

Gerald took an abrupt turn toward the river once they passed the walking bridge, knowing that Edwin's instructions would be true. He found a low place along the riverbank, climbed down to the edge, and tip-toed across several muddy sandbars to an area just below the low-water dam where the water churned regularly and kept the fish at a comfortable temperature.

"Have a look, Sam!" Gerald's eyes lit up. "Look at the size of those damned fish. We'll just need a few to make a meal! You jump over to that little sand bar and scare 'em my way!"

Sam wasn't eager to jump over the water but he swallowed his worry, then took a few quick steps and leapt across. He moved close to the water, making the fish take notice and saw them purposely move away from him and toward Gerald. Gerald wasted no time with the spear, quickly skewering the one closest to him and dumping it into the nylon bag. The doomed fish continued to flop about as Gerald removed the spear and searched for his next target.

The fish began to move more rapidly, sensing the danger, and Gerald missed on several thrusts.

"Step in a little closer now, Sam," he directed, "and I'll bag us another."

Sam took a few steps forward. Above the din of the frigid churning water, he thought he heard a familiar sound. The sound was pulsing and regular, but he couldn't place the noise. It must be the sound of all the cars on Riverside Drive, he thought.

Gerald skewered another fish, this one bigger than the first, fighting nobly with Gerald to stay in the water. Gerald focused and pulled the fish from the water, dropping it into the bag. He cinched the bag closed to keep the writhing pair of injured fish from flopping free.

Again, Sam thought he heard the familiar noise. It was interesting, he thought. Why did this noise register over the roar of the water and the excitement of the fishing?

Gerald thrust the spear again, snagging yet another pale white fish. He pushed this one in with the other two and cinched down the bag. As he pulled the string tight, Sam looked at Gerald's face just in time to see the blood drain from it and his expression turn to one of panic. Sam followed Gerald's gaze and saw the cause. Simultaneously, he realized that the familiar noise was the howl of the Corps of Engineers' siren. It was the same siren sound he heard while living in the culvert by the refinery, and it was signaling a rise in the river water. The muddy bridge of earth the pair had scampered across to arrive at this fishing spot was now well under water and their small muddy islands were shrinking quickly. Sam was now easily as panicked as Gerald.

Gerald looked Sam in the eyes, then looked down at the mesh bag of fish near his muddy feet. He watched the water coming up around his feet and smiled at Sam, "I guess we know how they feel, don't we! We're gonna have to swim for it. I hate to swim, and it's gonna be pretty damned cold in this water!"

Sam winced with pain as the water came up his legs. How did the fish live in this frigid stuff? He watched Gerald wade toward the riverbank as he breathed heavily in the darkening air. Then, as the water approached his chest, Gerald jumped forward and began to swim.

Sam jumped in the same direction, and tried to follow. The cold of the water took his breath away and he could feel the current of the river pulling him quickly downstream, but he kept straining toward the direction of the shore. Gerald went in and out of view as Sam bobbed in the current. He could see Gerald trying to hold onto both the spear and the bag of fish. Then, he saw Gerald drop the spear to swim. Then, he saw Gerald drop the bag to swim. Then, Sam saw Gerald no more. He looked for the man each time the current took him high, but he was not to be found.

Sam felt alone again. Moments ago he was catching dinner with Gerald. Gerald wasn't the companion that Ernest was, but he was there and they were working together. Now, Gerald was gone too. Sam hoped that Gerald was making it to shore, but didn't think it was likely. Like the fish in the bag, he knew that Gerald was in an uncomfortable place and couldn't get out of it.

Nonetheless, Sam continued to paddle his way through the cold and the current. The water was so cold that it hurt, and he quickly began to grow stiff. He thought he felt mud beneath his feet, but as soon as he had his footing, the current swept him into deeper water. He kept paddling, kept swimming, but his limbs were getting heavier and harder to move. As he became slower and slower, he began to wonder if he would make it to shore. He began to wonder if Gerald was better off. Surely he wasn't cold or hungry any more. Surely he didn't worry about having his dinner stolen or about being found by the authorities. Maybe it would be better for Sam to just stop swimming. He was tired enough, and every stroke took more willpower.

He was on the verge of letting the current take him when he saw the shadows of the trees lining the bank of the river and the endless line of red lights of the cars on Riverside Drive. Sam found the energy for a few more strokes toward shore, after which his feet found mud and somehow carried him up the bank to the river trail. He still saw the red tail lights of cars in traffic as far to the south as he could see, and was blinded by headlights as he looked to the north. He sat on the trail and tried to catch his breath. As he did, he found that he was shaking uncontrollably with cold. Despite his exhaustion and discomfort, all Sam could think to do was to run. Even with the shaking, Sam knew that he was fast on his feet. Maybe just maybe, he thought, he could outrun the cold and the evil grasp of the river. He faced toward the blinding headlights, knowing he had come from that direction. He started with a stiff limp, his muscles frozen from the river. Several minutes later, he passed the walking bridge. What had taken only moments in the current of the river had taken this long to run back up-stream. How long was he in the water? He took comfort in the idea that he knew he was getting close to the tent village, and was also comforted to feel his limbs under him, brought back to life by the brisk trot up the trail. He continued his jog, eventually finding the wide place in the trail and the park bench with the path leading to the clearing. He dashed toward the clearing, found his way to the tents and darted into Rosine's tent.

"Honey, you're soaked!" Rosine exclaimed as Sam made his clumsy entrance. "You couldn't get this wet from the mist out there! Let's get you and this yellow coat all dried out, or you'll be sick for sure! It's going to be awful cold tonight too! I hope Gerald made it back okay. It's too cold to be out wandering around."

The look in Sam's eyes let Rosine know that Gerald was not coming back.

"Oh, I'm so sorry, honey. I'm sure you both did what you could. Let's worry about what we can take care of for now, so we'll get you warmed up and dried off!"

Rosine dug some tattered towels from her pack began to pat at Sam's trembling body. Once he was dry, she layered blanket after blanket on him, finally wrapping herself in a thick sleeping bag and covering them both in the last of the blankets. She could still feel Sam shivering.

"Hold on, honey. We'll keep each other warm. You're dry now, and you'll warm up soon."

Sam felt comforted by the warmth and the companionship. He heard Rosine's breathing settle as she fell into sleep. His shivering eventually subsided, and he heard the mist outside change to a heavier rain, then into a mix of sleet and icy rain. The soft drops of water falling from the sky evolved into a sleet that klinked on the roof of the tent, getting louder as the freezing rain formed a layer of ice. His eyes eventually became heavy and closed for the night.

14. Cold

The pre-dawn glimmer from the street lights took on an eerie glow as it wiggled through the thin material of the tent's roof. Sam could still hear the klink, klink of the frozen water drops on the tent roof above him. It sounded almost like small pieces of breaking glass as it fell. He was surprised that there was no sound of traffic from Riverside Drive. The street had been packed last night. He listened intently for several minutes and heard no sound of engines or tires on the road at all.

He stuck his nose out from under the blankets to catch a breath and found the air so icy that it made his lungs ache. He exhaled, watching the fog spewing from his nostrils. He watched as the fog rose in the tent, not comprehending why the warmer air of his breath was rising in the colder air around it. That one breath was enough to convince him to put his nose back under the blanket.

He turned under the blankets to face Rosine. Her eyes were open, but her nose and mouth were covered for warmth as well. Sam could see the outline of her comforting smile beneath the blankets.

"It looks like we had quite an ice storm last night," she whispered, "Look at that the weight of that ice pressing down on my tent!" She moved her eyes to direct Sam's gaze to the roof.

Sam saw that the roof was sagging. It was inches below where it normally would have been, pressed down by the weight of the frozen rain. He was a bit startled, and Rosine saw the look of fear in his eyes.

"It's all right, honey, it's just a layer of frozen rain. The tent's okay for now. It might be pretty cold in here, but at least we're dry."

The way the tent sagged around its support poles made Sam curious enough to venture out from under the blankets. He pressed against a sagging part of the tent, expecting to feel the soggy wet texture of a saturated towel or blanket. Instead, he found the fabric to be stiff to the touch and incredibly cold.

"It looks pretty thick, and I can still hear it coming down," Rosine commented. "Let's see if Edwin is up. I'm sure he'll have an opinion about our situation."

Sam took a step toward the door, but Rosine called him back.

"No, Sam. Let's leave it closed and preserve what heat we have. I'll just holler. He's not that far off."

"Edwin! Are you up? Edwin!" Rosine's voice broke the rhythm of the freezing rain.

"I'm awake, but too cold to get up and around." Edwin's answer carried crisply between the tents, "Is Gerald with you two? I didn't hear him return last night."

"Honey, I don't think Gerald's coming back. Sam came back a tattered mess. I got him dried off last night, and am hopin' he won't catch a death of a cold today. If Gerald looked anything like Sam and didn't make it back here to get warmed up, then I'm sure he's found his way to his permanent home by now. I'm sorry, Edwin. I know he was your friend, and he was a great guardian to us both."

Edwin was silent. Sam could only assume that there was nothing for Edwin to say.

Rosine broke the silence with a practical question, "What'll we do about this frozen rain?"

"I think we should hope that it stops soon, or we won't be able to get out for some days. My tent is sagging on the poles. I hope it doesn't tear."

A staccato pop suddenly rang through the morning air, followed by several electrical zaps. Sam was startled, but judged the noises to be quite a distance off, so he didn't consider it to be an immediate threat. Directly after the racket, the street lights illuminating the morning fell to black, leaving the area completely dark.

"Well, that does it!" Edwin called. "It looks like even the rich neighbors are going to be living like us. No lights! No heat! Welcome to our world!" Edwin had a little grin in his voice, appreciating the fact that the even people dwelling in the houses would be subjected to some minor level of discomfort.

"Don't be snide," scolded Rosine. "You know it ain't right to wish ill on anyone, even if you have to bear that ill yourself."

"I'm not wishing ill on them," Edwin defended. "But I do take a little satisfaction in our shared suffering. There'll be some generators starting directly anyway. The real rich ones will have a contingency plan."

And, as Edwin had predicted, Sam heard small engines starting in the distance. He quizzically looked at Rosine.

"Yes, those are generators," she quietly confirmed for Sam. "We won't have street lights, and we won't have much traffic, but those folks will have the electric in their houses. How amazing is that?"

"It's still coming down," Edwin continued, "I am going to stay put for a while and see what daylight brings. I suggest that you do the same."

"Right there with you, Honey!" Rosine confirmed.

Sam gave the top of the tent one more nudge, just to feel the solidity of the ice, then crawled back under the blankets.

"Damn, it's cold out there!" Rosine commented, "It's a good thing that yeller coat of yours is dried off and keeping you warm. You'd be a goner without it."

Sam dug his mouth and nose back under the blankets and closed his eyes, trying to sleep while he waited for the sun to arrive. He hoped that the sun would bring a stop to this evil freezing rain and warm the earth so he wouldn't be trapped inside the tent. He listened to the sound of the rain, its sound so much different than the friendly rain he had walked through so many times with Ernest. This rain was quieter, yet it sounded menacing and felt mean. It gave off the sensation of a snake lying in the tall grass waiting to bite him. It felt to Sam like the rain actually meant to do him harm. While Rosine was acting calm and trying to make him feel comfortable, he could tell by the tone of her voice and the look in her eyes that she was truly worried about what the day would bring.

Not surprisingly, sleep did not come. Sam simply listened to the rain and listened to Rosine's labored breathing. Rosine wasn't as noisy as Ernest, but her breathing still required more effort than Sam thought was natural. Occasionally, he heard a curious snap coming from the sky, but he couldn't imagine the source of that sound. The klink-klink of the frozen drops continued as he watched the sky gradually lighten. While he couldn't see the light itself through the walls of the tent, he could tell that a thick layer of clouds was shielding the sun's warming rays from the earth. The freezing rain continued.

Rosine was stirring now. "OK, honey. I know you're wondering what it looks like out there, and I'm wondering too. Let's open the door a bit and take a quick peek outside. We just don't want let out too much heat, so look quick!"

Rosine crawled toward the zippered flap that she called the front door, and pressed her hand against the fabric.

"Pretty chilly!" She smiled and unzipped the flap a few inches, just enough to get a view across the clearing to see Edwin's tent. "Oh my! That's more ice that I thought! Come have a look."

Sam pressed his face to the hole, feeling the frigid outside air and taking in a sight that he could never have imagined. The clearing and the world around it sparkled, even in the weak light of this overcast day. Everything was covered with a shiny layer of ice. He could see the sag of Edwin's tent against its poles. All the grass and brush around the clearing was sparkling with the layer of ice. Even the stones surrounding the fire pit were shiny with the frozen water..

What struck Sam most as he gazed through the small hole was that the beauty of the scene was also sinister. He knew this was not right and that it presented a danger he didn't understand. He was frustrated that he didn't know what action to take.

"Edwin! Are you up?" Rosine hollered from behind Sam.

Sam saw the zipper in Edwin's tent open just enough for a set of eyes to peer out.

"Yes, I'm up!' the voice behind the eyes called back. "It's quite a scene out here, isn't it?"

Sam continued to look about, seeing the trees sagging under the weight of the ice clinging to their branches, some broken completely off, or hanging only from a thin strip of wood. The only noise was that of the rain, a handful of generators somewhere in the nearby neighborhood, and the curious snaps coming from the sky. Sam's eyes were drawn to a snap nearby, and he was now able to see that each snap was a tree branch giving way under the weight of the ice.

"This is not looking good," Edwin stated. "If this keeps up, we'll need to find a shelter for tonight."

"Edwin, you know that I ain't never going to sleep in another shelter. I know that'd be best for me, but I just cain't do it. I'd rather be cold all night than deal with being incarcerated like that," Rosine protested.

"Well, my dear," Edwin counseled, "we have the cold, the moisture and the potential for these tree branches to fall on top of us. It's looking pretty dangerous out here, and getting more so as this rain continues to fall."

Sam backed away from the opening, and Rosine zipped it back up.

"We'll just hole-up here for the day. I'm sure this freezing rain will stop soon," she said to Sam, struggling to sound calm.

They both huddled back under the blankets to keep warm. Sam tried to sleep, and tried to keep track of the day. He couldn't tell where the sun was in its trek across the sky. When he thought it was mid-day, he and Rosine took another look through the opened zipper. The rain was still falling, but with less intensity. He could see a good number of additional branches sheared from the trees surrounding the tents. The damage to the small forest around them was eerily impressive.

Sam was looking up at the trees when he heard a particularly large snap, and watched as the trunk of an oak tree by the fire pit split, sending half the tree across the top of Edwin's tent. As it fell, Sam watched the ice layers break off of the trunk and branches. Then, as the trunk smashed down on Edwin's tent, the veneer of ice shattered like a sheet of glass, sending clear shards of ice and frozen dust into the air with a mighty crash. Edwin's tent was largely hidden by the tree's branches, but what Sam could see was most certainly a total loss. Rosine heard the commotion and shoved Sam out of the way to look.

"Edwin! Edwin!" she called, "Can you hear me, Edwin! Are you all right?"

Sam could hear rustling from near the tent. He conceded to himself that it might be the branches of the fallen tree settling, but he hoped that it was Edwin working his way out of the tent.

"I'm here!" Edwin called back. "My tent's in a mess, though. I'm going to bundle up and head for the shelter. You should go with me."

"You know I'm not going to go. Don't bother to ask again," Rosine shot back.

"Suit yourself! Be careful and try to stay warm!"

Sam could hear Edwin rustling about, gathering up his important and portable things from under the twisted remains of his tent. After a bit, he heard the zipper of Edwin's door, and then a strange crunching as Edwin's shoes crushed the frozen grass as he stepped out.

Sam poked his nose out of the tent to have a look. Edwin was sensibly dressed with most all of the clothes he owned. He was almost unrecognizable beneath all the layers. He had one heavy pack, certainly not large enough to hold all his books and important study items, but large enough to be a heavy burden to Edwin. He slipped as he crunched toward Sam.

Rosine opened the zipper a bit more, poking her face out to bid Edwin goodbye as well.

"Rosey," Edwin said, worried, "I'm sorry I couldn't keep the electric on here. Even if I did, you know that we wouldn't have any since it's out all around us. Anyway, I know you don't want to, but you should come with me to stay warm. These clouds are pushing off to the south. That'll let the sun out tomorrow, but when they are gone tonight, it's going to get incredibly cold. The ice is bad enough, but the cold is going to be a killer. Why don't you come with me? I'll wait for you."

"Honey, you know I can't do that. I'm happy you're tryin' to take care of me, but I'm a *rough sleeper* at heart and I have to make my own decisions. I'll watch your stuff for you, and I'll see you in a few days. You be careful walkin' up that hill to downtown. If it's slick here, it'll will be slicker on the street. You know that's why there aren't any cars out there, right?"

"I'll be fine. You take care and keep warm," Edwin said, understanding that Rosine's decision was final. "You're a great person and I hope I'll see you soon," he called, as he managed a clumsy wave through his layers of clothes and began stumbling up to the trail. Sam heard him slip several times and curse loudly as he did. The sounds of the slips and curses grew more distant as Edwin pressed on, and Sam silently wished him the best. He could see that Edwin's concern for Rosine was sincere and well-founded.

"Alright, honey, we need to seal it up and conserve our heat. It's gonna be a long night." Rosine closed the zipper. "Let's get these blankets arranged, and hope that a tree don't break and fall on us. I'm starting to get a chill already."

The pair buried themselves below all the blankets, towels, and anything else they could find to cover themselves. The sun invisibly pushed its way over the western horizon and the twilight of the day faded into another pitch black night.

Sam closed his eyes and listened to the night. He was pleased that the threatening sound of the frozen rain was gone. In its place remained the sound of the frigid air moving through the frozen trees. The hardy branches and leaves that remained in the trees were still covered with ice and jingled like natural wind chimes as the gentle breeze flowed through. He still heard the occasional snap of branches breaking free, followed by a glassy smash as they hit the ground. He held his breath with each snap, praying that the falling branch did not start directly above him.

He looked up at Rosine, finding her eyes open and providing a clear window to see her growing worry. She started shaking shortly after they covered up, and while Sam had been able to find a relatively comfortable temperature, Rosine simply continued to shake with the cold. Sam moved closer to Rosine to share his warmth with her.

"Thanks, honey," she said, "I can use all the warmth you can share. I'm feeling pretty darned cold, but I'm sure tomorrow will be warmer. Hopefully, that old sun will melt all this icy crap away when it comes out tomorrow."

Sam smiled at Rosine, then closed his eyes. He was worried about Rosine, but he was more comfortable now than he had been for days, and he knew he could finally sleep.

The next morning, Sam woke to the light of a yellow sunrise, yesterday's clouds having blown away. He was pleased to see the light bathing the tent, but was shocked at how cold the air was around him. He looked at the blanket that had covered his face through the night and saw a layer of ice brought on by the continual freezing of his breath as he exhaled. He lifted the blanket to take a breath in the tent, and the cold air burned his lungs. If yesterday had felt cold, he didn't know how to describe this morning. He gingerly stepped to the zipper by the door and sneaked a peek outside the tent. He saw that the street lights were still not working, that no traffic was running on Riverside Drive, and he could still hear the generators in the distance. It sounded like the city would sleep again today.

Sam's attention turned to Rosine. Through the night, he could feel her shaking on occasion, continuing her labored breathing and sputtering out hacked coughs. But, looking down at her now, she appeared to be at peace. She was no longer shaking, and her rough breathing was silent. Despite the oppressive cold, Sam thought she would appreciate the sunshine, and so he gave her a nudge to rouse her. The nudge went without effect, so Sam escalated to a push. Still nothing. The push escalated to a violent shove. Still nothing. Pulling back the blankets to waken Rosine with the cold air, Sam finally realized that Rosine's breathing simply was no longer. The cold of the night had been the final push to take Rosine off the streets. The cold had taken Rosine home.

P.D. Bruns

15. Alone

Sam weathered the stifling cold, sharing the tent with Rosine's lifeless body, for three more nights. While he knew that he couldn't leave the safety of the tent without risking his own life, he was also extremely uncomfortable staying so close to a lifeless Rosine. The reflexes of her dead body made her suddenly move several times the first day. The noises and movements startled Sam at first. Then, they brought him false hope of her recovery. Finally, they just annoyed him as he realized that the twitches and groans were only the life continuing to leave her body. By the end of that first day, her skin was as cold as the wooden poles holding up the roof of the tent. By the end of the second day, her ears and fingers were frozen as solid as the ice covering the tent. There was no question that her life was gone.

Those first hours alone with a dead Rosine were filled with the roller-coaster of hope and despair and passed quickly. The days following seemed to take an eternity. The moon shone brightly through the first night, any blanket of clouds absent from preserving any warmth of the earth, and the light kept Sam awake until he could see the yellow disk of the sun peeking through the wall of the tent. The daytime sunshine brought a little heat into the tent, but Sam still buried himself beneath all the available blankets, and poked his face out only for short intervals to assess his situation.

He was left only to his own thoughts through those many hours, and those thoughts turned to the friends he had lost over the recent weeks.

Ernest had been the most significant, of course. His friend and mentor for nearly a year, Sam had played second only to Ernest's addiction to the Red Dawg booze. When Ernest wasn't influenced by the evil liquid, he had always been kind and thoughtful when showing Sam how to survive on the streets. Watching Ernest flail in the air after the collision was a memory that Sam would not be able to push from his mind, even if he wanted to do so. While he did treasure those last thoughts of Ernest, he worked to think of the good times that came before the traumatic collision.

Gerald, while he had been rude and vile to Ernest, was agreeable enough to Sam and was certainly an admirable laborer. He lost his life providing a meal for his friends. Sam had felt some sense of loss as he had wandered his way to the clearing without Gerald, but had not been close enough to him to feel a large hole in his life.

Now, still in the presence of Rosine's death, Sam contemplated the differences. Rosine was almost relaxed and peaceful in her departure. This was a significant contrast to Ernest's awkwardly bent frame. The quiet time in the tent was far removed from the awful noise from the torrent of water he heard envelope Gerald. Rosine had been quiet, only shuddering with cold as she went. Again, this was remarkably different from Ernest's cries of pain or Gerald's calls for help.

The method of death didn't really matter, however, since Rosine was just as gone as Ernest and Gerald. Sam was just as alone as the evening he had seen the car strike Ernest. In fact, he was even more so. At least when Ernest had gone,

Sam knew that he might be able to find a friendly face and land safely at the clearing. At this point, there were few well-defined options left for Sam. Further, if there were others that Sam might want to call on as friends, he was afraid that his very presence might bring about their demise as well. During Sam's time shivering beneath the blankets, he resolved that if he did not succumb to Rosine's permanent slumber, he would go it alone. He was happy to have had the comfort and companionship he had experienced, but the pain of the loss was just too much for him to go through again. Sam knew that he would have to work hard to survive alone. It would be only him. But he knew that he could do it and he knew that he would.

After that last cold night, Sam woke to the faint, familiar sound of automobile traffic on Riverside Drive. The significance of that sound didn't register at first; he had heard it so often while living in the clearing that it didn't really stand out. But, as his mind readied for the morning, he realized that the noise was the first sign of a world returning to some sense of normalcy. In the early dawn, Sam stayed beneath the blankets. He lay quietly and soaked in the sound of the city coming to life. The traffic noise set the tone for the early morning. Then, as the sun went higher, the noise of the traffic was obscured by the dripping sound of the snow and ice melting from the trees. The dripping continued to accelerate and took on the sound of a small brook.

Sam poked his nose outside the cover of blankets and found the temperature in the tent to be less painful than it had been the day before. The air was no longer so cold that it burned his lungs, and he saw the inside of the tent was now covered with liquid condensation instead of frost.

He stretched beneath the blankets, forcing the blood through his limbs, then he gingerly crawled out from beneath their insulation. While the lingering chill made him happy to have his yellow coat, he decided that it alone was enough to keep him warm and comfortable. He found his way to Rosine's stash of groceries and helped himself to some chips and lunch meat, awkwardly understanding that Rosine wouldn't miss the food. The ham and turkey was still partially frozen and the chips were quite soggy, but he was hungry enough that these inconveniences didn't slow him down.

His stomach somewhat satisfied, Sam ventured a peek outside the tent door. He was immediately blinded by the reflection of the sun on the shiny, snowy earth all around. Looking at the ground was almost as painful as looking directly at the sun. So, Sam squinted his eyes, almost closed, to get a better look around.

As the dripping sounds suggested, the frozen world around him was melting. The Oklahoma cold had disappeared as quickly as it had appeared, and now life was returning to the clearing. Sam looked across toward Edwin's smashed tent and judged that Edwin was wise to have left. The elements had certainly been threatening that night, but the crumpled tent would have offered little protection for any occupant, as its poles were pushed through the canvas by the weight of the tree and its branches.

There were fresh bird and rabbit tracks all around the clearing, suggesting that the wild animals of the urban forest were out long before Sam had stirred from beneath the blankets. The small animals' defiance of the danger of the cold gave Sam confidence to begin anew. He went back to Rosine's food stash, gorged himself on more soggy chips and half-frozen lunch meat, then set his mind to do what he knew he needed to do.

With his yellow coat as his only significant possession, Sam stepped from the tent into the brilliant light of the day. He took a final look back, knowing that he would not return to this place, and began his trek up through the reeds to the river trail. The snow and ice had smashed the foliage beneath its weight, so the campsite was now in clear view of parts of the trail. Sam realized that curious passers-by would soon make their way toward the tents, eventually finding the shell of Rosine's life. If he had been there for that find, it surely would have complicated his situation. There was no question that it was best for him to put some distance between the clearing and himself.

Sam started south on the river trail with no specific destination in mind. More than anything, he was curious about how the ice storm had changed the landscape of the city around him. He listened to the world as he walked, noticing the crunch of his footsteps on the ice that remained in the shady areas and low spots of the trail. The small-engine rumble of the generators was gone, replaced by an abrasive hiss of cars spewing dirty water as they traveled along the wet streets. Between the noisy packs of cars, Sam also heard the screams and giggles of children in the distance and decided to find their source of enjoyment in a time that he found to be so dismal.

Following the trail toward the sound of the giggles, then deftly jaywalking across Riverside drive, Sam saw a flurry of activity on a steep hill that led up to an opulent mansion, a remnant of Tulsa's oil boom in the 1920's. The hill was evidently a lawn area when not covered in snow and ice, as there were few trees on it, but on this day, several footpaths were worn into the snow, and there were smooth, shiny trails directly beside the foot paths. Sam watched from the bottom of the hill as the children climbed the footpaths carrying bright plastic sleds. After catching their breath at the top, they would jump head-first on the sleds, scoot onto the shiny paths, and move at harrowing speeds down to the bottom of the hill near Sam.

Sam was mesmerized and sat quietly and motionlessly on the cold snow watching the children. Adults, presumably the parents, milled about, mostly near the top. Some parents rode the sleds as well, but most kept their place as observers, chatting casually among themselves.

One small child received a friendly push from a parent, creating an even faster ride down the hill. The child squealed with delight as the sled bounced down the trail, eventually slowing to a stop just a few feet from Sam. Aside from the bright eyes and flushed cheeks, the child was completely covered from head to toe with a hat, mittens, thick boots, snow pants and what had to be several layers of clothing beneath its jacket. Sam couldn't tell whether it was a boy or girl, but he could tell that the child was grinning broadly and sweating profusely from the heavy clothing and repeated climbs to the top of the hill. The grinning child gave Sam a nod, then picked up the plastic sled and began a sprint back up the hill for another run.

Sam continued to watch as the child took turns with the others at the top. Sometimes the sled would bring the child close to Sam at the bottom, and other times the sled would overturn, sending the child rolling down the hill across the snow and ice. While Sam would have expected the child to complain about being rolled in the snow, the child seemed equally pleased to end the ride in a crash or in a long run to the bottom of the hill.

After a particularly long run ending near the bottom of the hill, the child turned to make the climb again, and Sam decided to follow for a different view. The path beside the sledding trail was well-worn from the foot traffic, but was still slippery in places. The child slipped on several occasions going up the hill, but kept a quick pace on the climb. Sam was sure footed and had no problem keeping up.

The top of the hill was a staging area of sorts, with winded children waiting their turn for one of the sled trails. Parents wandered about, doting on their broods and making sure they stayed covered in fabric, and occasionally digging snow or ice out of a child's jacket. As he approached the top, Sam noticed the number of eyes following him. The staring reminded him of his experience downtown and made him uncomfortable. The eyes of the children largely held curiosity, but the eyes of the adults varied between fear and contempt. It was obvious to Sam that the adults were not comfortable with his presence. Sam, while somewhat intimidated, still wanted to watch the scene from the top and so found a seat on a snowdrift between several children. Some parents continued to send their children down the hill, largely ignoring Sam's presence, but several others began to whisper between themselves, casting more glances toward Sam all the while.

Sam watched the sweating, bundled child he had seen at the bottom so many times take another run down the hill, cackling and squealing with joy during the whole trip. Like so many other times, the ride ended in a tumble creating a small cloud of white dust. The child then jumped up, straightened the hat on its head, grabbed the sled and started a sprint for the top. The child was understandably winded at the top of the hill, and walked close to Sam, smiling all the while.

The child gave him a friendly wave, and a giggly, "Hi there!"

No sooner had the words come from the child's mouth, then a mother scooped the child up, scolding her as if Sam wasn't even present. "Katie! Let's leave him alone. We don't know if he's friendly, and he looks like he might have some diseases. Let's go slide over here instead." The mother guided the child to another trail farther from Sam.

With that scene, other parents began to notice Sam's presence. After more whispers and stares in his direction, several fathers came close to Sam to encourage him to leave. "Hey, there, we don't need you around all these children," they prodded, "Why don't you run along now?"

Sam was taken aback at the words and their tone. What had he done that was threatening to anyone? Why would these people trouble him? Sam was not causing problems. He was simply sitting on the snow watching the sledding hill.

"Go on, now!" they continued, "You need to leave. You need to go now. Go find somewhere else to hang out."

Sam moved to another place to sit, hoping to keep his distance from these unfriendly types, but the gang followed him, picking up handfuls of snow as they came.

"You'd better get moving if you don't want to meet one of these snowballs!" one of the fathers yelled, but Sam obviously didn't move away soon enough and was smartly met across the face with a cold, wet clump of snow. It hit his nose and cheek, and his first reaction was to go on the offensive and jump out toward the threat. He realized, too late, that this further provoked the parents, and he suddenly found himself the target of a barrage of snowballs.

"Go on! Get out of here. We don't need you around these children," the throng shouted, continuing to throw snow at Sam while he scrambled out of range.

Once the snowballs stopped coming at him, Sam turned to assess the situation. He looked back at the mob of angry parents, most still with snowballs in their hands but knowing they couldn't throw far enough to hit Sam.

"Don't come back! Do you hear?" shouted the most vocal of the bunch, and several men threw additional warning shots toward Sam just for good measure.

While Sam had seen enough of the sledding hill and could tolerate moving on, he was completely confused by the reception of the parents. He still did not understand how he was considered a threat. He surmised that this must be how Ernest had felt when he saw his place among his own children. Sam now felt that he understood why Ernest would indulge in the Red Dawg during his sad times.

Not wanting to face the snowballs again, and not wanting to dwell on his feelings, Sam wandered down the neighborhood streets, finding the experience vastly different from his time in the downtown streets or in the clearing beneath the bridge. There were few people actually out walking, and those who were walking were armed with sleds, most certainly headed to the sledding hill. While his presence had been largely ignored downtown, the few individuals out and about here looked at him closely. Some appeared friendly and curious, but most faces held the fear or contempt he saw at the top of the sledding hill. Not one approached Sam in conversation. He wasn't disappointed by that fact, but did find it curious.

The sun had pushed through the clouds and was continuing its melting job on the streets and sidewalks. However, Sam knew that night would bring cold temperatures again and so he began searching for a suitable shelter for the evening. He wasn't comfortable coming close to the houses to look for a space below a porch or stairway, but did find a church on the edge of the neighborhood where there was just enough space between a concrete stairway and the building for Sam to slip between. In doing so, he made his yellow coat dirtier than it had already been, but he could feel the warmth radiating from the building and knew this would be a good place as long as he could be cautious with his coming and going. Once between the stairway and the building, there was just enough room for Sam to curl up for sleep or to turn around for a face-first exit. Sam was pleased with himself for finding such a place to stay. He knew that Ernest would have been delighted with the choice, and so Sam decided to make it his home.

Through the next weeks, Sam found himself to be satisfied living in the stairwell gap. It was well-sheltered, and only got a little wet when it rained. It provided shelter from the wind, and the main church building radiated the heat from inside. The church had regular gatherings and luncheons, making for a fairly constant supply of leftovers from day to day.

During the busy times around the church, Sam would stay beneath the stairs to remain unseen or at least anonymous. He would listen to the voices of the people coming and going. Most of the voices were certainly *rough sleepers*. They were mostly men, though he heard a few women as well. The voices were typically slurred and rough with an air of street-wisdom in the tone. But there were occasions when he would hear a very unique voice, a staccato voice of a man with clear speech and a very calm demeanor. That voice was often accompanied by other clear-speaking men and women, and even the occasional child. On those occasions Sam envisioned fathers and mothers guiding their children. Some might have been speaking sternly to children who had somehow misbehaved inside the building and appeared to be outside only long enough to incur their father's wrath before heading back inside.

Many of the voices became familiar to him, especially around the morning gatherings and the meal times. Sam would sneak a glance out from below the stairs to begin matching the voices to the parts of the people he could see. The staccato-voiced caretaker, as Sam thought of him, was a man who always dressed in black and had a particularly calming disposition. He was sought out by most all the other visitors, and appeared to have a kind word for each of them.

Sam also heard voices that appeared to be familiar. He felt that the repetition of living beneath the stairs caused them to sound familiar, but one in particular reminded him of his lost friend, Ernest. Sam listened for this voice whenever the people were coming and going. Sometimes he would hear it, sometimes not. Unfortunately, Sam wasn't able to see the man's face without risk of being seen, so Sam just imagined that it was Ernest coming to check in on him, to make sure he was doing well. The fantasy helped Sam cope with the loneliness. He recalled once thinking that others would be better away from him, but his need for companionship was pushing past that fear more every day.

During times between these meals and gatherings, Sam would wander to the south of the neighborhood to visit the restaurants near the Brookside district. He found that, while he was not welcome by restaurateurs or diners in the fronts of the shops, nobody seemed to notice when he found leftovers in the Dumpsters behind the shiny eateries. It reminded him of his time in the alleys in downtown, except there was less competition for the best morsels, and the trash bins were in a busier area shared with the customers' parking. This requiring Sam to be more mindful when doing his dinner shopping.

Brookside became busier as the days became longer and spring approached. The weather remained cold, but the young revelers either operated on the expectation that warmer weather was coming, or they had been inside for so long that they were willing to tolerate the chill. With the additional traffic around the area, and especially in the parking lots near the Dumpsters, Sam found it difficult to remain unobserved when approaching his food sources. Most of the patrons simply ignored his activity, or ostensibly kept their distance. However, there were occasional ruffians who called out to him and jeered as he explored the trash. Sam was confident that some of these patrons had notified the restaurants of his activity, as he began to find many of the bin lids closed more securely than they had been in the past. While Sam wasn't a genius, he was certainly crafty enough to get past the latches when he felt that there was something worth finding.

Only once did he feel a significant threat near the trash bins. It was on a cold but sunny day, a quiet afternoon without much traffic. Sam had found some leftover steak and potatoes in a bag near the top. As opposed to grabbing what he could and moving on to feast, Sam decided to dine in the Dumpster itself. After all, since the steak was so good, why move it away from the potatoes? He had finished about half the steak and was moving on to the next course, relishing the gravy, when the door to the Dumpster slammed shut and he heard the latch sound.

"I got you this time, you bastard!" shouted someone from the outside. "The trash truck will be here today and I'll not have to worry about you again! Goodbye, you dirty maggot!"

Sam understood the danger surrounding him. He had seen how the big trucks would empty the trash bins. The trucks struggled to lift them high above the ground, then they dumped the contents into the back of the truck. If the fall into the truck didn't kill him, the trash falling behind him would. Or, in the end, the noisy machinery inside the truck would finish things off. One way or another, Sam knew the needed to get free before the truck arrived.

Sam tried to open the doors, but they would not budge from the inside. He relentlessly called to the outside world, hoping a kind soul would open the door long enough for him to escape, but he was met with silence. He feared that every engine he heard approach was the trash truck ready to latch onto the dumpster, but many came and went and none lifted the large metal box.

Sam was too upset to finish the steak or potatoes, making the whole exercise a debacle now. He wanted to pace about, but there wasn't room inside. So, he scooted the bags around so he could get a firm footing near the door. Then he waited, hoping for just a tiny opening to leap from the box.

He could see the sunlight peeking through the cracks between the heavy metal door and the frame of the Dumpster. He watched the small sunbeam move as the sun slid down the sky making way for evening. Fortunately, the trash truck had not yet arrived. Maybe his captor had been mistaken about the truck coming that day. Hopefully.

Sam had mixed feelings at the end of the day. He only assumed that the sun had set, as the sunbeam that slid across the gap had finally disappeared and the metal box was growing colder. He heard footsteps approaching, and to his delight, a boy opened the door preparing to toss in three large black trash bags. Sam's muscles and joints were stiff from the cold and the cramped space, but he willed them to move and sprang from the box before the boy could react. Sam cleared the boy on the way out and did not look back as he made his way to his safe place beneath the concrete stairs at the church. He was surprised that he was happy to be back in a cramped space, but accepted the comfort with the knowledge that he could leave his stairway whenever he wanted. The Dumpster, on this day, had truly held him captive. That was not a situation that suited Sam's psyche, and was not an event he cared to repeat. Sam resolved to spend only the time necessary to gather food in the trash bins, and eat all his meals from a safe distance going forward.

As the Oklahoma spring began to bloom, Sam marveled at how he loved the season. The smell of the redbud blossoms tickled his nose when he walked near one of the trees. The rains became more frequent, and he even saw the first small hail storm of the year. He was happy to be protected by the concrete stairwell and the wall of the church. Even if he got a little wet, the ice balls of hail didn't fall into his space with any force and he was able to dodge most of the water. His place wasn't as luxurious as the Cincinnati Avenue Bridge, nor even the tent village in the clearing. However, Sam was comfortable and he felt almost at home in the environment. He stayed quiet while the people were coming and going from their church services. He even began to understand the ebb and flow of the church music, using the various sounds to know when to expect heavy foot traffic on the stairs and when the area around them would be quiet.

Several times, Sam believed the caretaker of the church had noticed his presence beneath the stairs. This was a mild-mannered gentleman, who was always dressed in black and was frequently having his hand kissed by others. The feeling that the he was aware of Sam made him uneasy. However, he had never approached Sam nor had he been threatening him in any way. Sam told himself that the man must not really have been aware of his home beneath the stairs. The caretaker was around the church all the time, even when the other visitors were not present. When the weather was nice, the man would sit peacefully in the garden, minding his own business and talking to no one in particular. It reminded Sam of his time with Ernest, at least the way Ernest would have conversations on his own. This man, unlike Ernest, would never raise his voice. Further, Sam had never seen the caretaker take a drink of the Red Dawg. Somehow, Sam felt comfortable that the man would not be a threat, even if he had noticed Sam's home.

On a day when the sun was warming the air and the church yard was quiet, Sam watched the caretaker come down the stairs and find a seat in the garden. The grass was wet from a short morning shower, so the man spread a dark towel before he sat. He crossed his legs, clasped his hands together, closed his eyes and began to speak to himself. Sam could not understand the words, but they were peaceful to him nonetheless. Sam watched from his shelter for some time, expecting the man to either run out of words or to raise his voice in anger. However, the caretaker simply continued in a low calm voice.

Curiosity pulled at Sam to the point where he drew up the courage to step forward from beneath the stairwell. He took a few steps toward the caretaker, still sitting with his eyes closed and still talking with himself, and took a seat closer with a better view of the scene. Sam knew that he was in full view of the man as well, but again did not feel threatened.

The caretaker's conversation became slower and slower until he was finally silent. Sam watched him breathe calmly. Then, before Sam could move, he saw the man's eyes open and focus on him. Sam caught himself in this error, and quickly jumped up, but the man did not stir. The caretaker calmly watched Sam's leap, and then a smile came across his face.

Again, curiosity pulled at Sam, and he held himself back from making a sprint away from the church. Surely this man would not be a problem for him, given that he was not springing to action against him. But, now that the man knew about Sam, what should he do? Sam could not bring himself to run.

"Hello there, my young fellow," the words glided from the caretaker's mouth, while his legs stayed crossed and his hands stayed clasped. "I've seen you about many times, and wondered if we might become friends at some point. I hope you're not afraid."

Sam did not know what to say.

"I'll tell you what, when you're ready to be friends, just let me know. We're all God's creatures, you know? As long as you don't make a mess around our Dumpsters and don't scare our parishioners, I'll not push at you and will try not to make you uncomfortable. OK? I know you need a place to stay, and that space by the stairs seems to fit you well. I'm sure it's not all that comfortable, but if it works for you, who am I to judge?"

With that, the caretaker rose calmly, smiled at Sam and walked right by on his way up the stairs back into the church. He passed so closely that Sam could smell the perfumed soap on his body. Sam surprised himself that he did not try to jump away. He could not believe that he fell so quickly under the trance of this man's calm. Yet, somehow Sam knew that the caretaker would cause him no harm.

P.D. Bruns

16. Going Home

The caretaker made more frequent trips to the garden as the springtime Oklahoma weather became more and more mild. The mornings were still a little frosty, but by mid-day the air was glorious. Sam began to look forward to the caretaker's visits to the garden. Every time he would come out, he would make a space to sit in the grass. Normally he stayed well away from any of the trees or flowers, choosing instead to have a wide area surrounding him. From there, he would calmly sit, cross his legs, clasp his hands, close his eyes and begin to talk. Sam knew that the caretaker could send him away whenever he chose, so he saw no real threat in coming out to watch the scene on a regular basis. Each time Sam watched, the caretaker's prayers would end with a period of silence. Then he would smile at Sam and make some small talk.

"We creatures of God are all imperfect," the caretaker would say, "and we need His help to get by. This is how I work to stay close to Him. I don't mind if you watch. I really don't even notice when you're there."

As the days passed, Sam found that he was comfortable coming to sit near the caretaker while he spoke with his God. While Sam didn't understand how or why the man chose to communicate in that way, it was evident that the man's time in the garden was always refreshing to him, and Sam could feel that the man held less anxiety at the end of his sessions than he carried into them. Sam didn't understand how the talking worked, but for this man it certainly did, and who was Sam to question?

While Sam wasn't interested in saying the words with the caretaker, he found that the man's feeling of peace and calm had an effect on him as well. When the man came outside, Sam would immediately move to sit near him on the grass and listen. Sam would find that he was more comfortable and relaxed after the prayer sessions, even though he had nothing to say. On stormy days when the man did not come to the garden for his prayers, Sam could physically feel something missing from his being. While it was still only early spring, he was already dreading the coming of winter when surely this good man would take his praying inside for several months.

"Well, my friend, I can tell that you've grown to trust me," the caretaker spoke directly to Sam after his time of silence this day, "And I am hoping that will continue. I have come to appreciate our time together, and hope that you enjoy it too."

"Now, then, do be aware that we have an important gathering later today," the man continued. "I have a special parishioner who has been away from his family for a very long time. He has been with us for some months, recovering from some medical problems, but God has seen fit to mend him well. Not only is he past his physical pain, but he has also taken control of some addiction demons that separated him from his loved ones. You know, what I find interesting is that this man frequently mentions having friends like you. He lived a lifestyle similar to yours for some time, and he made many acquaintances along the way. He seems happy to be away from the transient world, but I can tell that he worries that he may make an involuntary trip back there if his addictions come back to him. I hope that one day you can find yourself as this man did. He has gone through terrible physical and emotional pain in his recovery, but I think he feels it was worth the discomfort."

The caretaker took a breath and smiled at Sam, then said, "Anyway, today will be a busy day at the church, so you must remember our agreement. Please do not scare the parishioners, as I would hate to miss our time together like this, and I believe you would miss it too. There will be a lot of activity, so it will best for you to be scarce for most of the time."

Sam knew that he would miss the time with the caretaker should he no longer be allowed to stay at the church, and also knew that he could easily be stealthy this afternoon. It was how he operated on most days anyway.

"Now, while this man has frequently mentioned having acquaintances in situations like yours, he has also spoken more explicitly of having a friend very much like you. This would be a friend who would listen to him, accept him, and not judge him. He recalls a friend that was always willing to help, and asked for little more than a meal in return." He went on, "And I think you can relate. I think you could help this man and I think he could help you. So, at some point in the afternoon, I would like to introduce you to him."

The caretaker paused for a moment, sizing up Sam's reaction.

"I know that might be uncomfortable for you, but I think it might help you out as well. Also, it would give you an opportunity to help this man – one of God's creatures, just like us. I know you become reserved and silent when the crowds form, which is probably a wise thing for you to do. However, I would like to call on you at some point later today to make friends with this man. I will find an appropriate time, probably late in the event when most of the party has departed, to look beneath the stairs and request that you come out. If you are willing, please indulge me."

Sam was not sure how best to respond, and just looked back at the man in bewilderment.

Then, as was his normal process, the caretaker stood silently and gracefully moved past Sam. Again, he left the scent of his perfumed soap in his wake. Sam smiled to himself, though he wasn't sure why, and retired to his space beneath the stairs, thinking that another mid-day nap was just what he needed.

And yet, sleep would not come. He thought through this exchange. The man was calm and centered. He had been trustworthy and fair, yet now he was suggesting that Sam trust another. This was someone of whom he had no knowledge, but only the recommendation of the caretaker. Sam was not inclined to get close to this new person, and he realized that he need only stay below the stairs and out of sight to remain anonymous. Sam simply passed the afternoon below the stairs with only the company of his thoughts. He didn't sleep, but he didn't go out to move around either. He only wondered what interesting events the afternoon would bring his way.

Sam waited and listened, and the afternoon seemed to drag on. Finally, he heard the courtyard come to life as the sun started its fall toward the horizon. There were voices and footsteps above, much like he would expect on any busy church day. There was talking and laughing among the guests, and he could hear pockets of conversation beginning to break apart into men's, women's, and even children's voices. The pockets were spread around the courtyard, and Sam couldn't really focus on any of them. It was definitely the sound of a celebration, and it was getting louder than most of the post-church socializing that he was accustomed to hearing.

Sam sneaked a peek from his shelter to get a glimpse of the crowd. He was comfortable only taking a short look from a low place in the crack between the stairs and the church. From that low vantage point he found a sea of legs covered with flowery dresses and grey pants. The small talk and laughter continued as did the sound of children bouncing around the yard. However, the commotion faded as Sam watched the black-trousered legs of the caretaker walk to the middle of the crowd.

The caretaker began to speak, "Good afternoon everyone! We are so pleased that you are able to join us today for this special occasion. We feel fortunate that God has blessed us with such a beautiful afternoon, with the grass coming to life amidst the early-spring showers. The life around this courtyard is a testament to how life springs from the desolate winter, and it shows us how this kind of resurrection happens every year."

"Today, however," he continued, "we have another resurrection of sorts to celebrate. You see, we have a friend in our midst who has been dead to his family for some time. While this man has endured many hardships over the past couple of years, he also understands what hardships he has placed on his friends and family through that time. His recovery in the last months has involved not only coming to terms with his own addiction, but also recognizing that his family still loves him and would be there to support him during the recovery. He had to understand, for himself, that his family had always been watching out for him and wanted to help him come back in any way they could. He had to understand that, like God, his family could forgive him and accept him."

The crowd shifted as the caretaker continued his soliloquy. Sam wondered if he really needed to pay attention to all this conversation. He knew that the caretaker would come back to the stairs when it was time, so there probably wasn't any reason for him to listen to all this talking.

"We often find that others forgive us more readily that we forgive ourselves," the man continued, "and so we are called to take comfort in God's grace. While we cannot understand the full impact of the peace of God, we can understand that he forgives us and we can follow his example, forgive ourselves and enjoy a peace in that forgiveness. Sometimes we need another to lead us to that peace, and this was very true for our friend, Ernest."

Sam's ears were perked up, completely tuned in upon hearing that name.

"Ernest has battled alcohol addiction for years, and it eventually separated him from his productive life and his family. While his family continued to forgive him, he could not live with himself, and so exiled himself to living a transient life on the street. His wife continued to track him, from one shelter, tent or park bench to another. She sent food as she could afford, and when she could get Ernest to believe that it was coming anonymously. She tried…"

Sam could focus on nothing beyond the name he heard. Ernest! Could it be? Nothing else the caretaker said really made any difference at this point. This was the first time that Sam had heard that name in months. He was sure Ernest had died on that downtown street. Or, if he had not died, then surely the authorities had taken him away, never to be seen again. Certainly, this could not be the Ernest he knew standing in the courtyard.

Hope soon won out over sensibility and Sam found himself crawling from beneath the stairs, squeezing out from between the stairway and the church building. He stood and began to walk between the people gathered in the courtyard, knowing that his grubby looks and foul smell probably made it easier for him to part the crowd. People stepped back as Sam came through, and one mother quickly scooped up her toddler. The caretaker had warned him not to frighten the people. The man had been clear that Sam should stay hidden until he called. Sam knew that he should not come out, but he could not stay. He knew that it could cost him the shelter beneath the stairs, but at this point he did not care.

The parting of the crowd grew narrower and narrower as Sam approached the center where the caretaker was speaking. He saw the man's eyes meet his as he spoke, and saw the reproachful look grow, basically telling Sam to return to his place until he was called. Sam couldn't stop, however, he had to see who this Ernest was. He had to know.

As the last of the crowd parted, only a young family stood between Sam and the caretaker. The mother was stout, but not obese. She had two small children clinging to her, one on each leg, with the smaller one giggling as she clung. Beside her was a man, working to stand straight despite having to hold himself up with a pair of aluminum crutches.

Sam continued toward them despite the clear message in the caretaker's eyes. The caretaker continued his words until Sam was directly behind the man on crutches, and then he had no option but to acknowledge Sam.

"And so while I had planned to make this introduction a little later, Ernest, I would like you to meet one of our church guests. This guest and I have become better acquainted over the past weeks, and he reminds me of many of the stories you have related to me during your recovery, I…"

The man on crutches followed the caretaker's gaze and turned around on his weak legs to see Sam. Sam stared back, donning his soiled yellow coat and hanging his head low, standing in the crowd of people.

Sam's heart leapt in his chest as he saw that this was the Ernest who befriended him all those months ago. This was the same Ernest who taught him to survive on the street! This was his friend, who Sam thought was gone forever!

Sam's mind raced as he came to terms with this new reality. Ernest wasn't really dead. Here he was standing before him in this courtyard. The woman had to be Ernest's Shondra Lee. She had to be the woman that Ernest cried for beneath the stupor of the Red Dawg. But, if Shondra Lee had taken him back, Ernest couldn't be expected to come back to the street to stay with Sam.

Then, as if on cue, the woman turned around as well, and quickly stepped between Sam and Ernest, scooping the toddler up in her arms.

"You stay back, you dirty old scoundrel! You leave my Ernie alone!" she was still Ernest's protector.

Yet, Ernest hobbled close to his wife and put a hand on her shoulder.

"It's awl right, darlin'." Sam recognized Ernest's drawl, but noticed that it was clearer without the fog of alcohol in his system. "This here's mah ol' friend, Sam. We was good friends when I was livin' out thar, and we took care of each other."

"Well, that's all the more reason for him to stay away," she protested, "I want you as far away from that life as possible, you hear?"

"I understands, but yer see here, I'll bet that Sam here needs some help from us, and I'll bet I wouldn't have survived out thar without 'im."

With that, Ernest stepped beside Shondra Lee, lowered his crutches and bent down to sit. He set his crutches beside him as his oldest child then sat down on his lap. The toddler squirmed until her mother put her down.

Sam heard the danger in Shondra Lee's voice, and took some timid steps back from her. But then he saw Ernest, seated and non-threatening with children piled on top of him, do something that was a sure sign of their ongoing friendship. Now at Sam's level, Ernest extended his hand, palm down and allowed Sam to step forward and give it a curious sniff.

Sam knew Ernest's familiar voice, and confirmed the smell of his hand, but also found it interesting that his hand had acquired a bit of the perfume scent he detected on the caretaker. He also looked up into Ernest's eyes. They were filled with more life than Sam ever remembered, and some of the hard wrinkles on Ernest's face had begun to fade. Aside from the crutches and the limp, Sam thought that

P.D. Bruns

Ernest looked much better than he remembered from below the ramp in the parking garage.

The children giggled, giving Sam a start. Again, he took a step backward, warily looking up at Shondra Lee's disapproving face and the Father's surprised eyes.

"Oh, come on, boy!" Ernest worked to put him at ease. "Come on back over here. These kids will stay right here and won't scare you none, won't you kids?" he asked, more instruction to the children than a question.

Sam made his way closer to Ernest, and graciously accepted a firm scratching of his ears. Oh, how he missed that when Ernest was somewhat sober and they were living on street.

"Honey," Ernest looked up at Shondra Lee, "this here's one of the reasons I stayed alive on the street. He's a great dog, and loyal as hell. 'Scuse me, Father. Sam here helped me survive several times, bringin' mah squirrels and rabbits. But more than the food, he gave me a purpose out thar. He gave me somethin' ter be responsible fer. Helpin' take care of Sam helped mah understand that I could make mah way back ter you. We really need ter take 'im home with us. He'll warm up ter the kids too. Please honey? Please?"

Sam, having enough of the ear scratching, rolled over onto his back to accept a belly rub from Ernest. He could see that Shondra Lee wasn't elated about the situation, but she understood what he meant to Ernest. The silent gazes and broad smiles of Ernest's children lobbied heavily for Sam as well.

"Okay, Ernie," she smiled, "but he's going to need a good bath before he comes in the house. I want to see a real

228

yellow in that coat of his before he gets in my door. If we're gonna have a dog, he needs to be a blonde!"

Also by P.D. Bruns

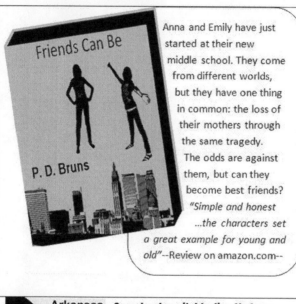
Friends Can Be is a young adult novel targeted for children ages 9 through 12. Set in present-day Tulsa, Oklahoma, the story centers on the blossoming friendship of two young ladies who share the tragic experience of growing up without their mothers. The circumstances of their relationship make their friendship unlikely. Yet, we are led through a story of discovery and forgiveness that shows human kindness in its purest form.

About the Author

P.D. Bruns is a long-time
resident of Tulsa,
Oklahoma, where he lives
with his wife and two
children. Having lived and
worked in many cities
across the U.S., Bruns has
found Tulsa to be rich in
history and culture, and
full of pleasant surprises.

Additional information about Mr. Bruns and his other
works is available at **www.pdbruns.com**.
Or, send a friend request to 'P.D. Bruns' on Facebook!

15462021R00139

Made in the USA
Charleston, SC
04 November 2012